For more than forty years,
Yearling has been the leading name
in classic and award-winning literature
for young readers.

Yearling books feature children's
favorite authors and characters,
providing dynamic stories of adventure,
humor, history, mystery, and fantasy.

Trust Yearling paperbacks to entertain,
inspire, and promote the love of reading
in all children.

OTHER YEARLING BOOKS
YOU WILL ENJOY

ALL ABOUT SAM, *Lois Lowry*

ALMOST STARRING SKINNYBONES, *Barbara Park*

MY MOTHER GOT MARRIED (AND OTHER DISASTERS)
Barbara Park

FOURTH-GRADE WEIRDO, *Martha Freeman*

IGGIE'S HOUSE, *Judy Blume*

JELLY BELLY, *Robert Kimmel Smith*

THE KID IN THE RED JACKET, *Barbara Park*

OPERATION: DUMP THE CHUMP, *Barbara Park*

SKINNYBONES, *Barbara Park*

SOUP, *Robert Newton Peck*

DON'T
MAKE ME
SMILE

DON'T MAKE ME SMILE

barbara park

A YEARLING BOOK

Published by Yearling, an imprint of Random House Children's Books
a division of Random House, Inc., New York

Yearling and the jumping horse design are registered trademarks of
Random House, Inc.

Visit us on the Web! www.randomhouse.com/kids

Educators and librarians, for a variety of teaching tools, visit us at
www.randomhouse.com/teachers

ISBN: 978-0-375-81555-3

Printed in the United States of America

First Yearling Edition February 2007

10 9 8 7 6

DON'T MAKE ME SMILE

(one)

THERE ARE certain things that happen to you that you never forget. I'm not sure why that is. But I know it's true. For example, no matter how old I get, I'll never forget the first time I was in a school program.

I was in the first-grade chorus. And since I was a very short first grader, I got to stand in the front row where everyone could see me.

Boy, I really thought I was hot stuff, too. I stood up there and sang my guts out. I even used my hands the way the singers on television do.

When it was all over, the audience started

clapping like crazy. It made me feel great. I must have bowed about two hundred times. Even while we were walking back to the room, I was still bowing.

I love going back to the room after a school program. You always get to horse around with the other kids until your parents come pick you up. The teacher tells you to calm down, but at night she doesn't really care. She only gets paid to keep you calm during the day.

Pretty soon, I saw my mother hurrying in the door. She was walking so fast, my father couldn't keep up with her. I could tell she was pretty excited about my performance.

Wow! I said to myself. I must have been even better than I thought. My mother looks like she wants my autograph or something!

As soon as she spotted me, Mom ran over and bent down beside me. I closed my eyes and got ready for one of her big fat kisses. But instead, she leaned over and whispered, "Charles, your zipper was down."

I looked down to see. And there, sticking out of my navy blue pants, was this big fat wad of underwear all bunched up in my zipper.

All I could think of was how stupid I must have looked on stage in front of all those people! How can you look like a big singing star with a bunch of underwear hanging out of your pants?

So I started to cry.

Okay, I know that there are a lot of first graders who wouldn't have cared one bit. They would have just zipped up and forgotten all about it. But that's not the kind of kid I am. To me, underwear is real private stuff. I don't even like my cat to see me in it.

After I fastened my zipper, I started yelling at my mother. Anytime you're upset, you're supposed to yell at your mother. They expect it. It's part of their job.

"It's all your fault!" I said. "You're the one who made me so short."

Mom tried to quiet me down. A couple of the other parents who had come in began to stare. Meanwhile, my father started looking around the room, pretending he didn't know me.

"Shh!" said my mother. "You don't have to shout, Charlie. And besides, what in the world does being short have to do with your fly being down?"

"Well, if you didn't make me so short, I would never have had to stand in the front row," I said. "And if I wasn't in the front row, no one would have seen that my zipper was down."

I guess I shouldn't have been talking so loud. Benjamin Fowler's parents started to laugh. My father left the room and headed for the car.

"Charles, *please*," said Mom as she hurried me out the door. "I'm sorry you're so upset about this. But I don't think it's fair to blame me just because you forgot to zip your fly."

"And stop calling it my fly!" I yelled.

Fly. Isn't that just about the stupidest name you've ever heard for a zipper?

My parents finally took me home and put me to bed. Before my father turned out the light, he gave me a little talk on zippers. He told me that being caught with your zipper down is just part of wearing pants. He also told me I would get used to it.

Well, he was wrong. I'm almost eleven years old now, and I'm still not used to it.

My mother says it's because I'm too sensitive.

Sensitive means that certain things bother you a lot more than they bother most people. For instance, whenever our family watches a real sad movie on TV, I'm always the first one to start blubbering. I try not to. But just when I think

I've got myself under control, someone in the movie goes and dies. That's when the blubbering starts.

Sensitive also means that you get your feelings hurt easily. I know this is true about myself. Sometimes, my feelings can get crushed over the least little thing. In fact, it just happened again a few weeks ago.

It was my father's birthday. And if there's one thing around our house I love, it's birthdays.

But this particular birthday was going to be even more special than any other. For the first time ever, I was going to get to buy Dad a present totally on my own. My mother said I could even keep it a surprise from her.

A few days before the big event, she drove me to the shopping center to buy his gift. She waited in the car while I ran in to get it. It didn't take long at all. I knew exactly what I wanted.

As soon as I got it home, I ran to my room to wrap it. I was afraid if I didn't wrap it right away, my mother might look in the box while I was in school. I don't mean to make Mom sound like a sneak or anything. But sometimes it's better not to test her.

I really can't explain why I wanted to keep this whole thing such a secret. I guess it just made it more special that way.

Anyway, when my father's birthday finally came, I couldn't wait for him to open my gift. When he started to unwrap it, my heart began to beat very fast. I felt kind of dumb getting so excited about it. But I just couldn't help myself.

Slowly, Dad lifted the lid of the box and peeked under the tissue paper.

I knew right away that I was in trouble.

"Oh, wow. Look at this," he said. "Gee whiz, Charlie. This is just great."

He didn't fool me a bit. Whenever someone opens a present and says, "Oh, wow. Look at this," it only means one thing. They don't know what it is.

Think about it. What do you say when you open up a new shirt? Simple. You say, "Oh, wow. A new shirt." And when you open up a new game, you say, "Oh, wow. A new game." But if you're not exactly sure what it is you're looking at, that's when you say, "Oh, wow. Look at this."

My father took his present out of the box and began examining it more carefully. He was trying his best to figure out what it was.

Finally, he unfolded it and put his hand

inside. "Oh, boy. I've always wanted one of these," he said.

It was so embarrassing I couldn't stand it.

"It doesn't go on your *hand*, Dad," I said at last. "It goes on your *head*. It's a chef's hat. You're supposed to wear it outside when you barbecue."

Dad laughed. "Oh, right! A chef's hat! Of course! A chef's hat!" he said.

He put it on his head. "Just call me Chef Boyardee!" he said in this ridiculous Italian accent.

By then, my mother was laughing, too.

I wasn't laughing at all. The reason I wasn't laughing was simple. It was not supposed to be a funny gift. If I had wanted to get a funny gift, I would have bought rubber vomit.

Anyway, by this time I guess my father could see that my feelings were hurt. He took off the hat and stopped clowning around.

He came over and hugged me. "Thanks a lot, Charlie," he said. "I really do like it. As a matter of fact, I think I'll barbecue tonight so I can wear it right away."

"Yeah, sure, Dad," I answered, trying to act cool. But inside, I felt awful.

Since then, my father's worn the chef's hat two or three times, probably. But I'm pretty sure he only put it on when he thought I was watching.

And if that's true, I guess I won't be seeing him wear it very much around here anymore.

Because two weeks after his birthday, my father moved out of the house.

He and my mother are getting a divorce.

DIVORCE—A DEFINITION

Divorce. To me, that word never really meant much. I think it's one of those words like *death*. You know that it happens to a lot of people, but as long as it's not you, you don't pay much attention.

As a matter of fact, I don't ever remember seeing *divorce* spelled before. I'm positive it's never been on any of my spelling lists at school. Come to think of it, neither has *death*. I guess you're supposed to learn how to spell all the sad words on your own.

I looked it up in my dictionary. It said: **divorce**/dih-vors'/n. 1. a complete legal breaking up of a marriage. 2. complete separation.

Well, that may be what the dictionary thinks divorce is, but I'll tell you what it really is.

Divorce is like watching your parents back

the car over your brand-new bicycle. You can see what's about to happen, but the car is already moving.

You shout, "STOP! STOP!" But no one hears you. So you just stand there and watch the tires of the car crush your bike as flat as a pancake. And you get this terrible, sick feeling inside you, like you're going to throw up or faint or something.

You cry, but it doesn't help. Your parents say they're sorry, but that doesn't help, either.

Nothing helps.

It's all smashed to pieces, and it will never be the same.

That's divorce.

(two)

SO FAR, one of the worst things about my parents' divorce is that I'm supposed to go around smiling all the time. When they were together, I never had to smile unless I felt like it. But ever since they split up, I have to keep looking real jolly and happy. If I don't, it makes them feel even guiltier.

"Cheer up. Cheer up." That's all my mother keeps saying. Then she tries to make me smile. If there's one thing I really hate, it's having someone try to make you smile when you don't want to.

"Come on," she says, "let me see a little smile."

Sometimes, I try to resist. But I know she won't leave me alone until I do it. So usually, I just shoot her a stupid grin to get her off my back.

My mother isn't the only one who keeps trying to make me smile, though. My father is just as bad. He even tried it the night he told me about the divorce.

He knocked on my door and asked if he could come in. I really could kick myself for not asking him what he wanted first. Then maybe he would have said, "I want to talk to you about the divorce your mother and I are getting." And I would have said, "Well, in that case, you can't come in. Not unless you promise to stay together."

And he would have said, "Okay. If you feel that strongly about it, I guess maybe we will." And then all of us would have lived happily ever after.

But instead, I just unlocked my door and let him in.

Dad walked over and sat down on my bed beside me. He had this real grim look on his face, like something terrible had just happened. It really got me scared.

"There's something very important that I have to tell you, Charlie," he said.

By this time, I was sure that someone had died.

I swallowed hard. "Was it Grandma?" I asked.

My father looked puzzled. "Was *what* Grandma?" he said.

"The one who died . . . was it Grandma?"

"Oh *no*, Charles," he said. "It's nothing like that. No one has died."

I felt relieved. "Thank God," I said. "For a minute there, you really had me worried, Dad."

"I'm sorry, Charlie," he said. "But still, what I have to tell you is very, very difficult."

As soon as he said this, I started getting scared all over again.

"I know that I'm not going to be able to explain this as well as I want to," he said. "But I'll do the best I can."

My father took a deep breath. "For a long time now, your mother and I haven't been very happy living here together."

"What do you mean you haven't been happy?" I said. "You always act okay to me."

"I mean that when your mother and I got married, we loved each other very much," he said. "And we thought that we would always feel that way. But sometimes things don't always work out the way we want them to. Even though two people care about each other, they're not always happy living together."

He shook his head. "They try, Charlie, but it just doesn't always work. And after a while they decide to make some changes so that they can both be happy again."

Dad stopped talking for a second and looked at me.

"Do you understand what I'm saying, son?" he asked.

"Sort of," I said. "You're saying that you and Mom need to do something to make yourselves happier."

"That's right, Charlie. We do," he said.

Now here is where I made my next big mistake. I asked an extremely stupid question.

"So what are you going to do?" I asked.

Man, I wish I had never asked that. If I hadn't asked it, maybe my father would never have said what he said. Maybe he would have changed his mind.

Instead, he waited a minute, then he lowered his voice and said, "We've decided to get a divorce."

I just sat there staring at him. I couldn't even speak, I mean.

Dad reached out and put his arms around me. He must have thought that I was going to start bawling or something. But I fooled him. I don't know why I didn't cry. I just didn't.

All I could do was stare.

Have you ever noticed that when you stare at somebody long enough, it makes them nervous? And when people get nervous, they say very stupid things. I know this is true. Because after I stared at my father for a while, he said the stupidest thing in the whole world.

"Are you okay?" he said.

I mean, just think about how stupid that is. Your own father comes into your room, sits down on your bed, and tells you that he and your mother are going to destroy your entire life. Then he asks you if you're okay.

Stupid. Stupid. Stupid.

As a matter of fact, it was such a stupid question, it deserved a stupid answer.

"Yeah, Dad. I'm fine," I said.

He ruffled my hair. "Of course you are," he said.

He stood up. "Well, I think I've told you just about enough for one night. I know this is going to be hard on you. It's going to be hard on all of us. But I don't want you to worry, Charlie. It's all going to work out fine. I just know it is."

He reached down and hugged me again. "How about a little smile just to show me you're okay," he said.

I shot him a grin to get him out of my room.

My father walked to the door.

"We'll talk about this again tomorrow, after you've had a chance to think about it. Good night, son," he said, closing the door behind him.

"Good night," I said back.

I waited a couple of minutes to make sure he was gone.

Then I ran into the bathroom and threw up.

(three)

I'M NOT sure how long I stayed in the bathroom that night. It was long enough to make my mother nervous, though.

She knocked on the door. "Charles, are you okay?" she called.

I don't know why she and my father aren't happy together. They both ask the same stupid questions.

"Great," I said. "I'm just great."

I looked in the mirror. I was so far from great it wasn't funny. My face was as white as a sheet.

I started the water in the tub. "I'm going to take a shower," I yelled.

"Well, if you need anything, just holler," Mom called back.

Oh, I do need something, Mother, I thought. I need two parents who care about me. I need you and Dad to stay together. But I didn't say it.

I stayed in the shower for over half an hour. I washed my hair twice for no reason. By the time I got out, my skin was so wrinkled I looked even worse than before.

I put on my pajamas and slowly opened the bathroom door. I wanted to make sure my mother wasn't hanging around the hall waiting for me to come out.

I just wanted to be left alone.

The coast was clear. I hurried into my bedroom and locked the door behind me.

"I'm going to bed now," I hollered.

But as it turned out, I didn't need to holler at all. When I turned around, my mother was standing there waiting for me.

I could tell she had been crying. Her nose was all red and her eyes were real puffy-looking. She looked awful.

I wanted to tell her to get out of my room, but I was afraid she would start crying again.

"Do you want to talk about it?" she asked quietly.

I didn't answer.

"Charles, please," she said, "I know this is a big shock for you, and it's very hard for you to understand. But it's hard for all of us."

A couple of tears rolled down her cheek.

All I can say is that if she was trying to make me feel better, she was doing one lousy job.

I wanted her to leave. It was all that I could think about.

I didn't say anything. I just unlocked my door and pointed to the hall. This clearly meant for her to go.

She didn't, though. She just stood there.

So I left instead.

I heard my father in the bedroom. I went to his door and looked in. He was standing there holding two suitcases.

Suddenly, I was furious. How could they do this to me? How could two people who were supposed to love me wreck my life like this?

My father looked embarrassed. "I guess I'll be staying in a motel for a couple of days," he said. "I'll come get you tomorrow and we'll talk. Okay?"

I just kept glaring at those suitcases.

He put them down and came over to me.

"Everything will be okay, Charlie," he said. "I promise you it will."

I backed away. I could tell I was making him feel uncomfortable. I was glad.

Finally, he picked up his suitcases again and walked out. "I'll see you tomorrow," he said.

I followed him down the hall to the front door. I wanted to make him feel as upset and sick as I was. I wanted to make him throw up, too.

As he headed down the front steps to his truck, I started to cry.

"Don't, Charles," he said. "Please don't cry."

Since he didn't want me to cry, I cried even louder. Making him feel terrible was the only thing that could make me feel better.

I really started to blubber.

There's a big difference between just plain crying and blubbering, by the way. Crying is when you make little whimpering noises and tears come out of your eyes. Blubbering is when you make this loud heaving noise, and your nose runs, and everyone in the neighborhood can hear you.

After my father put his suitcases in the truck, he reached out to me. I backed away again.

I didn't want him to touch me. All I wanted was to show him how terrible he had made me feel.

At last, he got in his truck and drove away.

I went back inside and ran to my room. My mother was still there. And to make matters worse, she was crying again.

She was really getting on my nerves. What in the world did she have to cry about? Her parents weren't splitting up, were they?

"I want to be alone," I said.

This time, she didn't argue. She just walked out.

As soon as the door was closed, I flopped on my bed. All I could think about was how both of them kept asking me if I was okay.

Suddenly, I got up and opened my door.

"And I'm NOT okay!" I shouted. "I'll never be okay again!"

(four)

WHEN SOMETHING bad happens, people don't all act the same way. Some people go nuts. Others just act like nothing has happened at all.

I always used to wonder which kind of person I was. Now I know.

I'm the kind who goes nuts.

I started going nuts the day after my father told me about the divorce.

My mother knocked on my door at the regular time to get me up for school.

"Are you awake, Charles?" she called.

I didn't answer. I must admit, I was getting

pretty good at not answering. It's really very easy. All you have to do is not open your mouth.

To me, the greatest thing about not answering is that no one can make you do it if you don't want to. That makes it very special. Because when you think about it, there aren't too many things your parents can't make you do if they really try hard enough.

Take mowing the lawn for instance.

One time I totally refused to mow the lawn. It was about a hundred and fifty degrees outside, and the grass was about a foot high. So when my mother told me to go out and cut it, I told her, "Later."

"No, not later, Charles," she said. "Now."

"No! Not now!" I yelled.

I don't usually disobey my mother like that. It's not that I'm afraid of her or anything. It's just that she can make my life pretty miserable if I don't do what she says.

Anyway, it only took about two seconds before Mom came into my room, yanked me by the arm, and pulled me outside.

After that, she started the lawn mower, put my hands on the handle, and put her hands on top of them.

Then, before I knew it, she was walking me all over the yard, making me push the mower.

Man, did I ever feel like an *idiot*. Every once in a while, one of my friends would ride by on his bike and laugh. It was totally humiliating.

Anyway, that's the kind of thing parents can make you do. But there's no way they can make you answer if you don't want to. No way in the world.

Of course, I don't want you to get the idea that I wasn't going to speak at all. Oh no. I was planning to speak, all right. But only when I felt like it. And only when I had something really mean to say.

"Come on, Charlie, get up," Mom said again. "I don't want you to miss your bus."

Can you believe that? She actually thought that I was going to school as if nothing had even happened.

Boy, was she in for a surprise.

I heard her go into the kitchen to start breakfast. But a couple of minutes later, she was right back at my door. My mother is like a boomerang, sometimes.

"Charlie, your breakfast is ready. Let's *go*," she shouted.

She waited.

"Charlie?" she called. "Charlie? ANSWER ME!"

Her voice was getting frantic. I think I know why, too. Since I hadn't answered, she was probably afraid that the stress of the divorce had been too much for me. Like she was probably thinking that I had had a heart attack from all the tension or something.

But not me. No way. In fact, just the thought of having a heart attack made me feel all spooky inside.

It also gave me a mean idea.

My mother got the key to my door and opened it as fast as she could. When she came into my room, I was lying there very, very still.

She ran over and pulled the sheet off me. "Charlie?" she shouted, shaking me. "Are you okay? Wake up! Wake up!"

I didn't move a muscle.

Mom hollered, "Oh my God!" and ran out of the room.

As soon as she was gone, I sat up and smiled.

A second later, she was back. Just like a boomerang.

When she saw me sitting up, she collapsed in relief. "Oh, thank goodness, Charles!" she said.

"I thought something terrible had happened to you."

She sat down on my bed and hugged me as tightly as she could. But my mother's not dumb. And it didn't take her long to realize that I had just played a very mean trick on her.

That's when she blew up.

Parents do this sort of thing all the time. As soon as they're sure you're not hurt, they think they have to punish you.

"Charlie! How could you do a thing like that to me?" she said. "How could you deliberately let me think that something bad had happened?"

I didn't answer.

By then, Mom had had it. She stood up. "Okay, I'm going to say this one more time, Charles! Get ready for school this minute. And I mean N-O-W!"

My mother is a very strange person. You'd think that when your kid is still wearing his pajamas ten minutes before the school bus comes, you would already understand that he wasn't going to school that day. But not my mother. She still wasn't getting the picture.

"I'm not going," I said at last.

She frowned. "Excuse me?" she said. "What do you mean, you're not going?"

I explained. "That means that I'm not getting on the bus. And I'm not getting off the bus. And I'm not going to my classroom. And I'm not sitting down in my seat. And I'm not going out for recess. And I'm not going to the lunchroom—"

Mom interrupted. "That's enough, Charles. That's really enough."

She walked around the room a few seconds. Then finally she sat down on my bed again.

Her voice was calmer now. "Look, honey," she said. "I know that you had an awful shock last night. And I know that you must be very upset about it. But that doesn't give you the right to go around acting horrible to everyone."

She continued. "Now, today, after school, your dad is going to pick you up and try to explain things to you better. There are a lot of things that he can tell you to help you understand what's happening. And sooner or later, we're all going to get through this. But it won't make things any easier if we all go around acting terrible to each other. Do you understand what I'm saying?"

I nodded.

"Good," she said. "I knew I could count on you. Now hurry up and get dressed."

"Mom?" I asked as she started for the door. "Could I just finish explaining what I started before?"

"Sure, honey," she said. "Go ahead."

"Well, I just wanted to say that after I don't go to the lunchroom, I'm not going to music. Then I'm not going back to my classroom. I'm not going to get dismissed. And I'm not going to wait for Dad to come get me."

Mom looked confused. "But you just said you were going."

"No, I didn't," I said. "I didn't say that at all."

My mother blew up again.

"Okay, Mr. Smart Aleck. Let me put it this way," she said. "You ARE getting dressed, and you ARE going to school! Do you hear me?"

I crawled back under my sheet.

Mom stormed over to my bed. "You listen to me, young man. I expect you to mind! I AM STILL YOUR MOTHER!"

Angrily, I looked up at her.

"No, you're not!" I shouted. "A mother is a person who *loves* her kids and who cares about their feelings. I don't know what you are, but if you ask me, you're sure no mother!"

This time, my mother didn't shout back. Instead, she ran to her bedroom and slammed the door.

I think I had made her cry again.

I don't care.

I don't like people who ruin my life.

(five)

THE REASON that I didn't want to go to school was simple. I didn't want to have to tell my friends that my parents were getting a divorce. I just didn't want to do it, that's all.

But refusing to go to school is a lot like mowing the lawn. If your parents really want you to go, they can usually figure out a way to make you. So while I was lying there in bed, I tried to think of what I would say to my friends if my parents made me go.

One thing was for sure. I didn't want to have to go around saying it a million times. I wanted to say it once and get it over with.

I wondered if our principal, Mr. Kabinski, would let me use the school intercom. The intercom would be perfect, I thought.

In my mind, I went over exactly what I would say.

May I have your attention, please? This is Charles Hickle speaking.

I would like to inform everyone that last night, at approximately 8:15 P.M., my father came into my room and told me that he and my mother are planning to get a divorce.

Now I know that some of you have already been through this sort of thing, and it didn't really bother you. But I also know that different people react to bad news in different ways. And as for me . . . I have gone nuts.

I hope this will explain why some of you saw my mother dragging me to school today. And I also hope it will explain why I am still wearing my pajamas.

I played it over and over in my head. It sounded pretty good, actually. But I knew I would probably never get to use it.

In the first place, I didn't think that my mother was strong enough to drag me to school all by herself. And even if she did, I was pretty sure that Mr. Kabinski would never let some idiot in his pajamas make an announcement over the intercom.

That's why I decided to try and think of another way to handle it. I mean, maybe I didn't have to be totally honest with my friends about the divorce. Maybe I could just tell them that my father had gone away on a business trip.

The trouble was, sooner or later, I knew someone would say, "Wow, your dad sure has been gone a long time. How long does this business trip last, anyway?"

Then I would have to say, "Oh, he's on one of those business trips where he never actually comes back."

And even though my friends seem pretty dopey sometimes, they're still smart enough to figure out that no one stays on a business trip forever.

Finally, there was only one thing left to do. I got out of bed and went into the kitchen to call MaryAnn Brady.

MaryAnn Brady lives next door. I don't like her very much, but sometimes she comes in handy. MaryAnn Brady is one of those people you can always count on to blab around your secrets. Like if you tell MaryAnn something totally private in the morning, she'll have it spread all over the school by lunchtime. Good old MaryAnn. It's nice to have someone you can count on like that.

After two rings, MaryAnn answered the phone. I figured she would still be home. MaryAnn doesn't take the bus. Her father drives her to school. I think she likes to stay home extra long in the mornings, just in case anyone wants to call with last-minute gossip.

"Hello," she said.

"Hi, MaryAnn. It's Charles," I said.

MaryAnn is also one of those people who doesn't say hi after you tell her your name. All she does is breathe.

"Listen, MaryAnn," I said. "I'm just calling to tell you that I'm not going to school today."

"So?" she said.

"So, I just wanted to tell you why I'm not going to be there, that's all," I said. "It's a big secret, though. I don't want anyone else to know."

I could almost see MaryAnn's eyes light up.

"What is it, Charles?" she said. "Tell me."

"Okay," I said. "But first you have to promise not to tell anyone. Not even your mother and father."

"I promise. I promise. Now tell me," she begged.

"Well, the reason that I won't be going to school today," I said, "is that last night my parents told me they're getting a divorce."

MaryAnn got so excited, she almost dropped the phone.

"What?" she said. "You're kidding? Your parents are getting a divorce? Oh my gosh, Charles! That's so terrible. A DIVORCE! Wow!"

Already I was sure that her parents had heard the news. Man, what a big mouth.

"I know, MaryAnn," I said. "But remember. You promised not to tell anyone."

MaryAnn didn't hear that part. She had already said good-bye. I guess she needed to hurry if she was going to tell the whole school by lunchtime.

As soon as I hung up, I headed back to my room.

Unfortunately, just as I started down the hall, my father walked in the front door. My mother must have called him to come help with my behavior.

"Charlie?" he said. "What's this I hear about you refusing to go to school today?"

I just looked at him.

Dad snapped his fingers. "Go get your clothes on, now," he ordered.

I don't know why, but when my father says to do something, it always sounds more *meaningful* than when Mom says it. And the funny part is, he doesn't even have to shout.

I went to my room and got dressed. At least now, if they dragged me to school I wouldn't be in my pajamas.

After I was ready, my father came in and sat down on my bed.

He put his arm around my shoulder. "Why are you acting like this, Charlie?" he asked. "This isn't like you. You're always so reasonable and easy to talk to."

I shrugged.

"What are you thinking?" said Dad. "Talk to me. I can't help you if I don't know what you're thinking."

I stared into space.

"Do you think that your mother and I don't care about you?" he asked. "Is that what you think? Do you think that we don't love you anymore?"

I shrugged again.

"Well, if that's what you think, you're

wrong," said my father. "Your mother and I love you very, very much."

Suddenly, I couldn't be quiet for one more second.

"Do you call ruining my life loving me?" I asked. "Huh, Dad? Is that what you call it?"

"We're not going to ruin your life, Charlie," he said. "It's not going to be like that at all. We're just changing things a little bit."

Now I was fuming.

"*Changing* things a little bit?" I yelled. "Do you call wrecking our whole family, *changing* things a little bit?"

My voice cracked, but I kept right on yelling.

"Do you call not having a father around anymore a little *change*? Or maybe you think that just because I'm a kid I'm too stupid to know what divorce really means. Maybe you guys think I'm too dumb to know that my whole life is wrecked."

My father shook his head. "Charlie, no. We've never thought that you were stupid."

"Well then, why do you go around asking me stupid questions, like whether I'm okay or not?" I asked. "Because for your information, I am *not* okay, Dad. I'll never be okay again."

I flopped back on the bed and buried my face in my pillow.

My father didn't do anything for a while. He just kept sitting there.

Finally, he told me I didn't have to go to school. He asked if there was anything that he could do for me.

I raised up a little. My throat ached from holding back the tears.

"Yeah," I said. "You can move back in with Mom and me."

He closed his eyes a second, then left.

(six)

STAYING HOME from school never turns out to be as much fun as I think it will. Usually I get so bored, I end up wishing I had gone in the first place.

The next day, I decided to go back to class. When I got to my room, I was very proud of MaryAnn Brady. Just as I predicted, everyone already knew about the divorce.

The first person to mention it to me was my teacher, Mrs. Fensel. She walked over to my desk and lowered her voice.

"MaryAnn told me about your problem at home, Charles," she said softly. "If there's anything I can do to help you, please let me know."

It made me feel embarrassed. "Yeah, sure . . . okay . . . thanks a lot," I mumbled.

At lunchtime, I hurried to find the table where MaryAnn was sitting and slid in next to her.

"Congratulations, MaryAnn," I said dryly. "You really did a great job yesterday."

"Congratulations for what?" she asked.

"For being such a big blabbermouth," I said. "Thanks to you, the whole school knows about the divorce."

MaryAnn looked at me a second. Then she said exactly what every single blabbermouth in the whole world always says right after they finish blabbing a secret.

"I didn't tell anyone. I *swear*," she said.

"Yes, you did, MaryAnn," I said angrily. "You know you did. Why can't you just learn to keep your big trap shut?"

I wanted to make sure that she thought I was really mad about it. Blabbermouths only like to tell secrets if they're not supposed to. If MaryAnn Brady ever found out that I actually wanted her to blab some of the stuff I told her, she'd stop doing it. And like I said before, sometimes she can come in handy.

"I didn't tell, Charlie. I didn't," she insisted.

"Well then, how come about a thousand people came up to me this morning and told me that they knew all about the divorce?" I asked. "And how come they all said it was you who told them? How do you explain that, Blabbo?"

"Anyone who told you that is a big fat liar," said MaryAnn.

"Oh really, MaryAnn?" I said. "Gee. I'm sure Mrs. Fensel will be glad to know that you think she's a big fat liar. Because when I got to school today, Mrs. Fensel told me she knew all about my 'problem.' And she also told me that she got the news from you."

I got up from the table. "Excuse me for a minute, Blabbette," I said. "I think I'll go tell Mrs. Fensel that you think she's a big fat liar."

MaryAnn's face turned pale as a ghost's.

I walked over to the table where Mrs. Fensel was eating lunch. MaryAnn watched me as I tapped my teacher on the shoulder. Then I whispered something in her ear and pointed to where MaryAnn was sitting.

You should have seen MaryAnn squirm. She

packed up her things and ran out of the lunch-room.

I didn't see her for a while after that. But someone told me that she had run into the bathroom and started to cry.

I don't know what she was crying about. All I had done was show Mrs. Fensel where I was sitting and ask her if I could have a few extra minutes to eat my lunch. I told her I was having a hard time swallowing.

It wasn't a lie, exactly. Being upset always makes it hard for me to swallow.

Of course, lately, I hadn't had to worry too much about swallowing when I was home. After Dad left, the meals that my mother made were so terrible that I didn't even want to go to the table.

I probably should have reported her to the health department or something. I think there's a law to make mothers feed their children good dinners. If there's not a law, there ought to be.

The first week that my father was gone was the worst. I remember when Mom called me to supper the first night. I was really getting hungry. I had spent the whole day in my room thinking about how ruined my life was. For lunch I had only been able to eat half an apple. I wanted more, but I just couldn't get it down.

Anyhow, when I went to the table that night, I thought that I had made a mistake. Maybe it wasn't dinnertime, after all. The only thing on my plate was a hard-boiled egg and two slices of bread.

"Didn't you just call me to supper?" I asked Mom.

"Yes," she answered. "Sit down and make yourself an egg sandwich."

The thought of eating a dried-up egg sandwich made me sick. I'd rather eat a frog.

"Don't we have any soup?" I said.

"Listen, Charles," said my mother. "Don't give me a hard time, okay? Please, just eat your sandwich and drink a glass of milk. I'll make you a better dinner tomorrow night."

She kept her word, too. The next night, she made one of those macaroni and cheese dinners out of the box . . . and the next night . . . and the next night. . . . As a matter of fact, my mother cooked macaroni and cheese dinner four nights in a row.

I used to like macaroni and cheese a lot. Now I can't stand the stuff. It's just one more thing that this divorce has ruined for me.

The whole idea that my mother wasn't cooking anymore really bothered me. It's not that I wanted to eat. In fact, usually I didn't feel much like eating at all. It's just that I thought she could have tried a little harder. When she didn't try, it made me feel like she didn't care.

The fifth night she served macaroni and cheese, I finally told her how I felt.

"What are we having for dinner tonight?" I asked, as if I didn't know.

Mom stirred it in the pot. "I'm heating up that leftover macaroni and cheese," she said.

"Don't we have any soup yet?" I asked.

"I told you before, Charles. I'll get some next week," she said. "I just haven't felt much like going to the grocery store. And besides, I thought you loved macaroni and cheese."

"I used to," I said. "But that was before I ate three million macaronis in a row. Come on, Mom. Can't we just go to the store and get some chicken noodle soup?"

"No, we can't," she said. "Not tonight." Then she plopped a big spoonful of macaroni and cheese on my plate.

I pushed it away. "No, thank you," I said. "If I put one more little macaroni in my mouth, I'll gag."

I felt myself getting mad.

"I'm not a pig, you know, Mother," I said.

"What in the world are you talking about?" she asked. "I never said you were a pig."

"I mean I'm not a pig, and you can't just throw some slop at me and expect me to eat it."

My mother got furious. Mothers really hate for their dinners to be called "slop."

"Go to your room!" she snapped.

I stormed out of the kitchen and hurried to my bedroom.

By then, I was in the worst mood ever.

Angrily, I gathered some of my things together and stuffed them in an old shoe box. I would have stuffed them in my old gym bag, but it got broken at Harold Stengler's spend-the-night party. Harold and another kid were trying to zip me inside it when the sides busted.

I spotted my dumb helicopter beanie hanging on my bulletin board. My father had bought it for me at the state fair a couple of years ago. It's probably the corniest thing I own, but for some reason it always makes me laugh.

I snatched it off the bulletin board and stuck it on my head.

I figured if I ever needed a good laugh, it was now.

Then I picked up the shoe box, opened my window, and left.

(seven)

RUNNING AWAY from home is something that I'd always wanted to try. I would have tried it a long time ago, but I never had a good enough reason. Until the divorce came along, my parents had never done anything bad enough to make me leave. I mean, once in a while I got sent to my room. And a couple of times they took my allowance away. But that's about it. I always thought it would sound stupid if I had to tell my friends that I ran away from home because my parents wouldn't give me the five bucks they owed me that week.

But divorce . . . now *there's* a reason to run away.

When I climbed out my window that night, I've got to admit, it was a pretty big thrill. Being out alone after dark is an exciting feeling. It makes you feel real sneaky, like a cat burglar or something.

I started walking down the street very slowly. I didn't run. When you run away from home, the worst possible thing you can do is actually run. Running makes you look like you're doing something wrong. Personally, I think they ought to call it *walking* away from home. I bet a lot less kids would get caught if they knew they should walk.

The most important thing about leaving home is that you've got to have a plan. If you don't have a plan, you might as well stay put.

As for me, I've always known exactly what I would do if I ever left home. I got the idea from a TV show I saw a couple of years ago.

The show was about these two little kids who ran away from an orphanage. They didn't have anywhere to go, so they decided to live in a tree in the park. It turned out to be perfect, too. No one found out about them for months.

When I got to the end of my street, I turned and headed toward the park. We only live about three blocks from there, so it didn't take long at all. And once I arrived, finding the tree I wanted to live in was simple. I chose the one next to the boys' bathroom.

It was a big tree with low branches, so I figured it would be pretty easy to climb. I held the shoe box under my arm and started up. I've always been a pretty good tree climber. My legs aren't very long, but I have great balance.

After I got up about ten feet, I stopped to look down. It was perfect. The limbs were so thick and bushy, I knew no one could spot me.

I picked out a nice fat branch to sit on and put the shoe box on my lap. I lifted the lid and looked inside. I had packed three pairs of underpants, a toothbrush, a pair of pajamas, and an old comic book.

"Oh, man. What stupid stuff to pack," I said right out loud.

I sighed. Oh, well, it didn't really matter, anyway. The important thing was that I didn't have to eat macaroni or listen to any more divorce talk.

I thought about my mother and wondered

what she was doing. By now, she had probably discovered I was missing and called the police. I wasn't worried, though. Not even the best detective in the world could have spotted me in such a thick tree. I was completely safe.

I leaned back and tried to make myself comfortable. Since it was too dark to read my comic book, I decided to figure out a way to sleep. On the TV show I had seen, the kids had built a tree house. I would start on that soon, but right now I had to do the best I could.

The first thing you need when you're trying to get comfortable is a pillow. I took my shoe box and placed it between my head and the tree trunk. I tried to pretend it was soft.

"*Ahhhhh*," I said. "Now that's more like it."

It wasn't any use, though. I've never been much good at pretending. The shoe box didn't feel at all like a pillow. It felt like a shoe box.

I would have used my pajamas for a pillow but I needed to use them as a blanket. It had really started to get chilly. Even though it was April, it felt more like January. This gave me one more reason to be angry at my parents. If they really loved me, they would have waited until July to get divorced.

I tried scrunching up into a ball to keep

warm, but it didn't help. Finally, I took two pairs of underpants out of the box and wrapped one around each hand. When I get cold, my hands are always the first part of my body to freeze. Next come my ears. And this time was no exception.

I had no choice. I took off my beanie and put it in the box. Then I pulled out the last pair of underwear and put them on my head. I pulled them way down so they would cover my ears. I never thought I would do anything that dumb. But when you're as cold as I was, you don't care if you're dumb.

It wasn't long before I started shivering. In science, Mrs. Fensel had told us that shivering is the way your body tries to warm itself. Well, I'm sorry to tell her, but she's wrong. Shivering makes you feel even colder. There's no way that you can hear your teeth chattering together and convince yourself that you're getting all toasty warm. No way.

"Brr!" I said. "Brr, brr, brr!"

When you're freezing, saying brr is about all you can do.

I promised myself that the next morning, I would sneak home and bring back a blanket. Meanwhile, I tried not to think about how cold and uncomfortable I was. The main thing was that I was out of the house and no one could find me.

"BRR!" I said louder.

"Cold up there?" asked a voice.

I panicked. Who said that? Who was down there?

I got very quiet and listened.

"Yooo-hooo," said the voice, again. "I see you, Charlie Hickle."

No. This was *impossible*. No one could have possibly seen me in that tree. Carefully, I looked through the branches. It was dark, but I could see someone's shadow.

"Charrrrrrlie . . ."

Oh no! It was my *mother*. But how could that be? There was no way she could see me through branches that thick. I was sure of it.

Wait a minute, I thought. Maybe she's just bluffing. Yes, of *course*. That was it! When my mother found me missing, she came to the park and started calling my name. She was hoping that I would give myself away.

"Hey up there," Mom called. "You with the underwear on your head."

She wasn't bluffing.

This was, without a doubt, the most embarrassing thing that had ever happened to me. It was even worse than singing in the chorus with my zipper down.

"Go home!" I yelled. "Leave me alone!"

"Don't be silly, Charlie," she said. "You can't stay in a tree all night. If you don't come down, I'm going to call the fire department."

Geez. She was treating me like a cat.

"Go home," I yelled again. "I mean it, Mother! I'm going to live up here for a while. And stop treating me like a cat."

"For heaven's sake, Charlie. You're being ridiculous!" she shouted back. "You can't live in a tree. Just think about how crazy that is. How will you keep warm?"

"I'll shiver," I said. "I learned it in science."

"Oh, wonderful," said Mom. "And what exactly do you plan to eat?"

"Nuts and berries."

Right away, I wished I hadn't said that. Now I sounded like a squirrel.

"This is absurd," said my mother. "You leave me no other choice, Charles. I'm going to go call the fire department to get you down."

She started to walked away. I didn't really think that she would call the fire department, but there are some things you just don't want to risk. And having a big hook-and-ladder truck come drag you out of a tree is one of them.

"Okay, okay!" I yelled. "You win. Don't call the fire department. I'm coming."

I started down the branches. On the way, I remembered to grab my pajamas and my shoe box. Unfortunately, I didn't remember to take the underwear off my head.

When my mother saw me, she started to laugh. She tried not to, I think. But let's face it, I looked like an idiot.

"I'm sorry, honey," she said, pulling it off my head. "I know you must be freezing."

She put her arm around me, and we began walking home. For once in her life, she didn't start lecturing me.

When we got to the house, I headed for the front door, but my mom grabbed my hand and walked me to the car. We both got in.

She drove to the grocery store and gave me some money.

"I'll wait here," she said. "Go get as many cans of chicken noodle soup as you want."

On the way home, we stopped at Burger King and got a couple of Whoppers.

By this time, I was feeling better about things.

But I was still very curious about how Mom had spotted me in that tree.

"So how did you do it?" I asked at last. "How did you know where to find me?"

"It was simple," she said. "I followed you."

"You *followed* me? You mean that you were behind me the whole time and I didn't even know it?" I asked.

"Yup," she said. "When I heard your bedroom window open, I went to see what you were doing. Just as I looked in your room, you were climbing out. So I followed you."

I rolled my eyes. "Man, some cat burglar," I mumbled.

That night, when I got in bed, I have to admit it felt a lot better than the tree. I fluffed my pillow like never before. Those poor squirrels don't know what they're missing.

My mother came in to say good night. She finally gave me the lecture on how we're supposed to talk about our problems, not run away from them. She said if there was anything else bothering me, I should share it with her.

Well, I hated to tell her, but there was a *lot* else bothering me. I still didn't feel like sharing it, though. That is, except for one thing.

"Mom," I said as she was leaving.

"Yes, Charlie?" she answered. "What is it?"

"I just hope we don't have chicken noodle soup five nights in a row, either," I said.

My mother shook her head and shut the door.

(eight)

THE NEXT day was Saturday. It was the first Saturday since I had learned about the divorce.

Usually on Saturdays I get up early and start calling my friends to find something to do. But this time I didn't feel like it.

I stayed in bed until my mother called me for breakfast. I wasn't hungry, but I could tell by the smell coming from the kitchen that she had made something special. I think she was still trying to make up for all the macaroni and cheese.

When I got to the table, I saw that she had fixed French toast with cinnamon and sugar. It's one of my favorites.

"Sit down and eat, honey," said Mom. "Your father will be picking you up in a few minutes."

This was news to me. I hadn't even seen my father since Monday morning.

"What's he picking me up for?" I asked. "I wish someone had asked me first. I might not feel like being picked up."

The more I thought about it, the more annoyed I got.

"It really makes me mad when people go around picking me up when I don't want to be picked up," I said again. "It's just inconsiderate, that's all."

My mother tried to reason with me. "Charlie, it's really time that you and your dad had a chance to talk," she said. "He's been waiting all week to speak to you. But he wanted to let you settle down before he came over."

"What makes you think that I'm settled down?" I asked. "If I was settled down, do you think I would have run away to live in a tree? Does that sound like a kid who is settled down? I don't want to see him."

"Well, I'm sorry, but I guess it doesn't matter whether or not you want to see him," said Mom. "He'll be here any minute."

A few seconds later, the doorbell rang. I can't

tell you how weird it is when your own father starts ringing the doorbell of his own house. It makes him seem like a deliveryman.

My mother hurried to let him in. When she came back to the kitchen, she kissed me on the cheek and left right away. It was pretty clear that she didn't want to be in the same room with Dad and me. I knew exactly how she felt. I didn't want to be in the same room with us, either.

My father was the only one who was acting happy. He came bouncing into the kitchen all smiles.

"Good morning, Charlie," he said. "Mmm. What smells so good in here?"

"French toast," I muttered.

"French toast? Mmm. Do I love French toast!" he said.

"Oh," I said. "Too bad you don't live here anymore. Then maybe you could have had some."

I held a big bite out in front of him. It was dripping with maple syrup. I stuffed it into my mouth.

My father could plainly see that I wasn't settled down. He stopped being quite as cheery.

"Let's just try to get along today, okay?" he

said. "I've got a nice little trip all planned for us."

Oh no. Not a dumb little trip. I couldn't stand it. It was going to be just like on TV. On TV, whenever parents get divorced, the father always gets the kids on the weekends and takes them on stupid little trips. They almost always end up going someplace real corny . . . like the zoo.

"We're going to the zoo," said Dad.

Geez. I knew it. Just like on TV. Well, no thanks . . . not me.

"I don't like the zoo," I said. "The smell at the zoo makes me puke."

My father looked disappointed. "Oh, come on, Charles," he said. "We'll have a great time."

"The zoo is for babies," I said. "What's so great about seeing a bunch of stinking animals?"

Dad didn't answer. As a matter of fact, he hardly said another word. But after I finished eating, he took me by the arm and led me to the truck.

I didn't really think that after all the mean stuff I had said he would still want to take me to the zoo. But I was wrong. We went to the zoo anyway.

As soon as we got out of the truck, I sniffed the air and held my nose. My father ignored me. He paid at the gate and we went in.

I made some gagging noises. People began to stare. You'd have thought that they'd never seen anyone smell stink before.

Dad walked over by the lake where all the peacocks hung out. I followed. When he sat down in the grass, I just stood there.

"Sit, please," he said.

"No, thank you," I said. "Bird poop."

"Excuse me?" asked my father. "What are you talking about?"

"I'm talking about the big pile of peacock poop you just sat in," I told him.

Dad jumped up and looked at the grass.

I smiled. "April fool."

My father was losing his patience. When he sat back down, he pulled me with him.

"I'm tired of your little jokes, Charlie. I'm tired of the way you're acting. And most of all, I'm tired of trying to be nice," he said. "If you know what's good for you, you'll shape up right now."

He went on. "There are a couple of things I want to talk to you about. And the first one is about where you're going to live," he said.

"Your mom and I aren't quite sure what to do with you."

"Nice," I said. "Why don't you just give me to Goodwill? Isn't that what people do with stuff that they don't want anymore?"

Dad rolled his eyes. "I didn't mean it that way and you know it," he said. "Now could you please stop feeling sorry for yourself long enough to listen to me? Who said we didn't want you?"

I shrugged.

"Charlie, the trouble is that we *both* want you," he said. "Believe me, no one is trying to get rid of you. As a matter of fact, I was just going to ask you if you would like to come and live with me for a while. I'd really like to have you, and I could sure use the company."

I have to admit this took me totally by surprise.

"You mean you already have a place of your own?" I asked.

"I've got an apartment," he said.

"Where?"

He stood right up. "Come on, let's go. I'll show you."

We left the zoo and drove for about fifteen

minutes. We finally stopped in front of a dumpy old building. I was hoping we had just run out of gas or something. But no such luck.

"Well, this is it," said Dad. "What do you think?"

I kept looking around. "What do I think about what?" I asked. "All I see is that dump over there."

My father looked annoyed. "That 'dump' is my apartment building," he said. "A friend of mine owns the building, and he rented me the apartment on the second floor."

Some friend, I thought.

I had already decided that I didn't want to live there. In fact, I wasn't even sure I wanted to go inside.

My father opened my door and led me around back to the stairs. We climbed to the second floor. When he unlocked the door to the apartment, he had to give me a little shove to get me to go in.

I took a whiff of the place.

"Phew. What's that smell?" I asked.

I think the question hurt his feelings, but I couldn't help it. The place smelled worse than the zoo.

"It's just a little musty," he said. "It hasn't been used in a long time. But after I air it out and give it a paint job, I think it will be fine."

Suddenly, I didn't feel quite as mad at my father as I had been before. For the first time, I began to realize that he and my mother must have been pretty unhappy together for him to end up in a stink hole like this.

I sat down on the couch. But I didn't stay there long. I think that's where the stink was coming from. I got up and moved to the chair. The smell wasn't much better there. But since I had run out of furniture to sit on, I stayed put and tried not to breathe.

My eyes roamed around the room.

"I just don't get it, Dad," I said. "I mean, if you and Mom were this unhappy, how come I never heard you guys fight?"

This was something that had really been bothering me a lot lately. I think if my parents had gone around screaming at each other all the time, I might not have minded if they got divorced. But they always acted so normal with each other, I never even knew anything was wrong.

Dad thought a minute. "When two people are unhappy, they don't always scream and fight,

Charlie," he said. "Your mother and I aren't screamers. In fact, what we did was probably even worse. We just shut each other out."

He continued. "It's so hard to explain what happened to us, son. I'm not even sure we know ourselves. Your mom and I started out loving each other very much. But over the years, our feelings for each other changed completely."

"But why?" I asked. "Why did you let your feelings change?"

"We didn't mean to," he said. "It happened so slowly that we hardly even realized it. All we knew was that after all these years, the fun of being together just wasn't there anymore. But it wasn't until a few weeks ago that we finally sat down and talked about how deeply unhappy we've both been."

My father shook his head. "I wish that we had talked about it sooner," he said. "Then maybe we could have stopped what was happening to us. But we didn't. And now it's too late."

"No, Dad. It's never too late," I told him. "You're always telling me that a person can do anything if he really wants to badly enough."

"Yes, Charlie. But in our case, that's *exactly* the problem," he said. "Neither of us wants to try.

Your mom and I want to stay friends. But we don't want to stay married to each other. We both know that for sure."

After that, my father and I sat there for a long time. I didn't want to admit it, but part of me understood what he was saying. The same kind of thing had happened to me and a friend of mine.

A few years ago, this kid named Andy Roberts moved in across the street. At first, I was really happy about it. Andy and I became instant best friends. We did everything together. My mother said that we were more like twins than just friends.

But after a year or so, Andy started getting really interested in insects. It seemed like every time I went over there, all he wanted to do was collect bugs and put them in jars. He kept telling me it was a *fascinating* hobby. Seriously. He must of said the word *fascinating* a million times. I mean, I have nothing against insects, okay? But after you've put a few bugs in jars, it gets pretty boring. All you do is watch them crawl up the sides and then knock them back down again. Real *fascinating*.

Anyway, we never fought or anything. I just stopped going over there. And now mostly all we do is wave at each other from across the street. I don't hate Andy or anything. And I don't think he hates me. I guess it's like my father said. We just changed too much to hang out together.

After a few minutes, Dad walked over to the smelly chair where I was sitting.

"So, how about it?" he said. "Do you think you might want to live here with your old pop?"

I didn't want to hurt him anymore. But there was no way in the world that I was ever going to move in there.

"Um, well, I don't know . . . maybe it would be better if I just stayed with Mom for right now," I said. "She's probably going to need my help around the house a lot more than you will."

I crossed my fingers and hoped that she hadn't told him about how I'd run away from home the other night. When someone runs away, it doesn't actually make them sound that helpful.

Dad looked at me. "That's true, Charlie. She will be needing your help," he said. "But what she doesn't need is for you to keep acting up. She told me that you ran away last night."

Good old Mom. The woman can never keep anything to herself. I bet when she was little she was an exact copy of MaryAnn Brady.

"I'm not going to run away anymore, Dad," I said. "I swear."

"I certainly hope not," said my father. "I'm not going to have you making things worse for your mom. If you're not happy there, you are always welcome to come live here with me."

Dad looked at his watch.

"Okay, now that we're straight on things, how about some lunch?" he asked. "Are you hungry yet?"

I wasn't, but I nodded anyway.

He walked over to his little kitchen. "I'm actually getting to be a pretty good cook," he said.

He reached into the cabinet above him and pulled out a box.

It was macaroni and cheese.

(nine)

WHEN MY father brought me home that afternoon, I said hello to my mother and went straight to my room. I wasn't sure why I was in such a hurry to get there. But as soon as I closed my door, I started to cry.

It was really weird, too. I didn't even know I was going to do it. And the worst part was, I couldn't stop.

My father was still in the house. He heard me and came in to see what was wrong. I asked him to leave me alone.

When he left my room, I heard him tell my mother that it might be good for me "to get it out of my system." They didn't bother me after that.

This was the first time that I had cried in almost a week. In fact, until then I hadn't even felt like crying, hardly. I guess I had been more mad than sad. But after seeing my father's apartment, it all started sinking in.

Every time I thought about it, I cried even harder. I know this makes me sound like a total wuss. But I don't really care. I think when you're sensitive, you have more crying in you than other kids.

All I know for sure is that when my mother called me for dinner that night, I couldn't eat a thing. I just sat there looking down at my food and sniffling. It was too bad, too. She had made fried chicken.

I tried to make her feel good by eating a few bites, but it was no use. I couldn't swallow. I just sat there with chicken in my cheeks. Finally, Mom told me I could come back later if I was feeling better.

I went back to my room and cried a little more.

That night I must have even cried in my sleep. Because the next morning my pillowcase felt soggy.

It was Sunday, and there wasn't much to do. I got up for a while and wandered around the house. But I kept ending up back in my room, thinking about my mom and dad.

By late that afternoon, my mother was getting worried about me. The only time I had come out of my room was to get more Kleenex. She made me some homemade soup and brought it to my room. It was real nice of her and all. But I couldn't eat it.

I went to bed early. I thought maybe if I got a good night's sleep, I would feel better in the morning. But when the morning came, I still felt lousy. My mother must have sensed it, because she let me stay home from school again.

About nine o'clock, my father dropped by to see how I was doing. At least, I thought that's why he came by. Actually, he had another reason. And it turned out to be a very sneaky one.

"Could you get your clothes on, Charlie?" he asked.

I shook my head. "No, Dad. Please. I can't go to school today. I don't feel good," I said.

Anyone could see that I wasn't faking.

"I know you don't, Charlie," said my father. "But there's somewhere else I'd like to take you this morning. Just get ready, all right? It'll be good for you."

As I was getting dressed, I convinced myself that he was taking me out to breakfast. For some reason, even if I don't have an appetite, the thought of blueberry pancakes usually cheers me up a little.

We drove for several miles. Finally, Dad pulled up in front of a small white building.

"Come on," he said, getting out of the truck. "There's someone in here I'd like you to meet."

It didn't look much like a restaurant. I was getting suspicious.

My father and I went inside and headed down a long, narrow hall. When we were almost to the end, he stopped in front of one of the offices.

"Well, this is the place," he said.

I looked at the sign on the door. It said:

DR. HENRY T. GIRARD
Child Psychologist

A shrink? Oh no. Not a shrink! I couldn't believe he'd brought me here.

"Why, Dad? Why did you do this? What a sneaky trick!" I said.

I started to back up, but my father grabbed me by the arm.

"Just talk to him one time, Charlie. That's all I'm asking," he said. "He can help you feel better. I know he can. If you don't want to come back after today, you won't have to."

Quickly, he pushed open the door. The secretary at the desk looked up and smiled.

"Good morning, Mr. Hickle," she said cheerfully. "This must be Charles."

My father nodded. "Is Dr. Girard ready to see him?"

"Yes. He can go right in," she said. She pointed to a door across the room.

Dad knocked twice, opened the door, and gave me a nudge. "I'll be out here if you need me," he said.

Dr. Girard was sitting at his desk. He wasn't very old for a doctor. When he stood up to greet me, I could see that he was wearing faded jeans and a sweater. I don't know why, but that really surprised me. I didn't think doctors were allowed to wear jeans to work.

"Hi, Charlie," he said, smiling. "I'm Henry Girard."

I didn't smile back. As a matter of fact, I didn't even say hello. I just sort of stood there feeling like a fool. I still couldn't believe that I was talking to a child psychologist. It made me feel all weird inside. Like I was a nutcase or something.

"Please, sit down," said Dr. Girard.

I sat.

He sat, too.

"Do you know why your father brought you here today?" he asked.

"Not unless you serve pancakes," I said. "I thought he was taking me out to breakfast."

Dr. Girard laughed. "Sorry," he said. "But I have a hard time just making cereal."

"Yeah, that's what I was afraid of," I told him.

"Oh, believe me, Charlie," he said. "There's nothing here to be afraid of. Your dad just brought you here because he knows that you're really unhappy right now. And he's hoping that maybe I can help."

I didn't reply. I didn't know what I was supposed to say. I had never been a nutcase before.

Dr. Girard sat down in his chair. "So do you want to tell me what's going on at home?" he asked.

"No, not really," I said.

I wasn't trying to be rude. It just felt weird

talking to some strange man I didn't even know. I mean, all your life your parents go around telling you not to talk to strangers. Then all of a sudden, they decide to get a divorce, and boom . . . they dump you in some strange guy's office and they expect you to spill your guts out.

I looked around some more. "Where's the couch?" I said. "Aren't crazy people supposed to lie down on a couch when they talk to you?"

Dr. Girard laughed again. "Well, I don't get many 'crazy' people in this office," he said. "But you're not the only one who thinks that you have to be 'crazy' to come here. At first, almost everyone I see thinks that."

I had to admit, the guy was trying to be understanding. But even so, he was still a stranger.

"It probably feels funny talking to a stranger about your problems, doesn't it?" he said next.

Great. Now he was reading my mind.

"I promise you, Charlie. You won't have to tell me anything that you don't want to," he said. "In fact, all I would like for you to do is answer one small question for me. It's a question I ask all my patients. Are you ready?"

I nodded.

"Okay, here's the question," he said. "How do I look?"

Geez. What a stupid thing to ask.

I didn't answer. If you ask me, answering a stupid question is almost as stupid as asking it.

Dr. Girard stared at me.

"I'm serious, Charlie. How do I look?" he asked again.

I was going to try to outstare him, but I figured he was probably a lot better at staring than I was. After all, he got to stare at people all day long. So finally, I gave in and answered the stupid question.

"You look fine," I said. "Can I go now?"

Dr. Girard laughed some more. For a guy who worked with nutcases all day, he sure laughed a lot.

"Do you think you could be a little clearer?" he said. "I mean, do I look happy to you? Or depressed? Or mad? How do you think I look?"

I shrugged my shoulders. "I don't know. I guess you look happy."

"You're right," he said. "I am happy."

Well, goody-goody for you, I thought. Why was he acting like such an idiot all of a sudden?

Personally, I didn't care whether he was happy or not. All I wanted to do was get out of there.

Dr. Girard kept talking. "The thing is, though, I wasn't always as happy as I am right now. As a matter of fact, Charlie, when I was your age, I was just about the most miserable kid that you've ever seen in your life."

I knew he was setting me up. He wanted me to ask him why he used to be miserable. I tried not to, too. But my curiosity got the best of me.

"Okay. I give up," I said. "Why were you miserable?"

"For the exact same reason that you are," he said. "I was miserable because my parents told me they were getting divorced."

I should have known he was going to say that. He was trying to find a way to get me to talk about my own situation. It was sneaky, I thought. But it wouldn't work.

"As a matter of fact," continued Dr. Girard, "I was so unhappy about the divorce that I did something pretty strange."

Once again, my curiosity got to me. What could he have done that was any stranger than the things I had done? What was stranger than going to live in a tree?

"So what did you do?" I asked.

"I stopped speaking to my parents," he said.

I rolled my eyes. That was it? He honestly thought that not speaking to your parents was *strange?*

"No offense, Dr. Girard," I said. "But what's such a big deal about not speaking to your parents? I stop speaking to my parents all the time."

"For a whole year, Charlie?" he asked. "I didn't speak to either one of my parents for a year. Not one word."

Now I felt insulted.

"Oh, come on," I said. "I'm not some dumb little kid, you know. I understand what you're trying to do here. You're trying to get me to talk by making up a bunch of wild stories. No one can stop speaking to their parents for an entire year."

Dr. Girard leaned over his desk and looked me straight in the eye.

"One . . . whole . . . year," he said again.

This time, I could tell he wasn't kidding.

"But that's impossible," I said. "How could anyone stop talking for a whole year?"

"Wait. Hold it. I didn't say that I stopped talking, *completely*," he said. "I said that I stopped talking to my parents. I talked to everyone else just fine. My friends, teachers . . . everybody, except Mom and Dad."

"Wow," I said. "My mom and dad get mad if I clam up for even a couple of days. What did your parents do?"

"They did exactly what your father did today," he said. "They took me to a child psychologist. In fact, they took me to a bunch of psychologists. But it didn't do any good. I was a very stubborn kid. I would talk to the psychologists as friendly as could be. Then I'd go home and not say another word."

This was unbelievable. "So let me get this straight," I said. "You didn't say one single word to your parents at all? Nothing? Never?"

Dr. Girard shook his head. "Nope. I mean once in a while, when they asked me a question, I would shake my head yes or no, but that's about it. I never opened my mouth. Not even at Christmas."

"So you didn't ask for any presents?" I asked. This guy was amazing.

"Not one," he said. "And believe me, that turned out to be a very big mistake."

"Why? What happened?" I asked.

"Well, that Christmas I really wanted a

basketball hoop and a stereo," he said, "but since I wasn't speaking, no one knew it. I thought about writing a Christmas list on a piece of paper, but I decided that would be almost like talking, so I didn't do it.

"Anyway," he continued, "when I got up on Christmas morning, all I found under the tree was a game of Life, a ton of school clothes, and some handmade mittens."

I started to laugh.

"Wait. That's not the worst part," said Dr. Girard. "My mother put fruit in my stocking. Two oranges and an apple. She knew I'd hate that. I'm sure that's why she did it."

I laughed even louder.

"Take it from me, Charlie," he said. "If you ever decide to stop talking to your parents for any length of time, wait until after the holidays."

"Don't worry," I said. "I could never last as long as you did. I always think of too many mean things that I want to say to them."

Dr. Girard nodded. "Well, sometimes, that's okay," he said. "Sometimes it's better to say what's on your mind—even if it's mean—than to keep everything inside."

I shrugged. "I don't know," I said. "I've said plenty of mean things to them already, but it doesn't seem to be helping me that much. I still feel just as rotten as I did when they first told me. Maybe even rottener."

The doctor thought a minute. "Tell me something, Charlie. When did you first find out about the divorce?" he asked.

"Last Sunday night," I said.

Dr. Girard looked surprised. "Last Sunday night? But that was only a week ago."

"Yes, I know," I said. "It's been a whole week, and I feel just as bad now as I did then."

He leaned forward. "But that's what I'm trying to tell you," he said. "A week is no time at all, Charlie. If you're thinking that you should feel better in only a week, you're in for a very unpleasant surprise. It takes time to get over something as big as this. Lots of time."

"I understand that, Dr. Girard," I said. "But every day I seem to feel even sadder than the day before. I think I'm getting worse instead of better."

He shook his head. "Let me try to explain something to you," he said. "What if last Sunday night, instead of finding out about the divorce, you'd had an accident. Let's say that you fell off your bike and you broke your arm. Okay?"

"Okay," I said.

"Well, if last Sunday night you fell off your bike and broke your arm, would you expect it to be healed by today?"

"No," I said.

"No, of course you wouldn't," he said. "Because you know that broken bones take lots of time to heal. But what a lot of people don't know is that there is another part of us that can take even longer to heal than broken bones. And that is our emotional part, Charlie. Our hurt, broken feelings."

I sighed. "No, you don't get it, Dr. Girard," I said. "It's not just my *feelings* that are hurt. This is a lot worse than that. Hurt feelings happen when your father puts his chef's hat on his hand instead of his head. I can get over stuff like that. I do it all the time."

Dr. Girard looked puzzled. But I didn't feel like explaining the chef's hat thing, so I kept on going.

"My parents are ruining my whole *life*," I said. "It's like they've wrecked every part of it. And nothing will ever be the same again."

"Like what?" asked Dr. Girard.

"Like *everything*," I said. "You ought to know. Like the three of us will never take a vacation together again. And on Christmas morning, it will only be Mom and me. And whenever I have something special to tell my dad, I'll have to call him on the phone. Before, when I had something to tell him, I used to just listen for the sound of his truck pulling into the driveway after work. But I can't do that anymore. Because he won't be coming home anymore."

"It doesn't seem fair, does it, Charlie?" said Dr. Girard quietly. "You're not the one who caused any of this, but you're the one who's feeling all the hurt."

Suddenly, I felt tears coming into my eyes. It's embarrassing as anything to cry in front of strangers. I kept my head down so he couldn't see.

"Do you have a Kleenex?" I asked. "I think there's something in my eye."

Dr. Girard handed me a whole box of tissues off his desk. I blew my nose.

"I must be catching a cold," I said.

Finally, I looked up. "So how much time do you think it will take before I feel better?"

"I won't kid you, Charlie," he said. "It's not

going to be quick. But there are certain things that you can do to help speed things along."

"Like what?" I asked.

"Like telling your parents what you're thinking, and not keeping your feelings all locked up inside of you like I did," he said. "Keeping everything in only makes it hurt worse."

"Yeah, well, like I told you before, I've already said some pretty mean stuff."

"I know. But remember," he said, "there's a big difference between 'telling' your feelings and 'yelling' your feelings. Eventually, you're going to need to start talking to your parents more calmly about things, Charlie. Calmly, but *honestly.*"

He stood up. "I'm here every day. Monday through Friday, plus most Saturdays. If you ever want to talk to me again, just give me a call and we'll set it up. I mean it, okay? You can call me anytime."

He reached out to shake my hand. Whenever a grown-up shakes my hand, it always makes me self-conscious. I never know how hard I'm supposed to squeeze. If you squeeze too tight, a lot of grown-ups will make some dumb comment, like, "Wow, that's quite a grip you've got there, tiger!" I hate it when they do that.

Anyhow, this time I must have squeezed just right, because Dr. Girard didn't comment at all.

When I left the office, the secretary gave me a card with his number on it. I shoved it in my pocket.

My father came over and put his arm around me. We walked outside to the truck.

"So how did it go?" he asked. "Are you still mad at me for bringing you?"

At first, I wasn't going to speak to him. But then I thought about what Dr. Girard had said about honesty.

"I think it was really rotten for you to bring me here without telling me, Dad" I said. "At least you could have been *honest* about it. I thought you were taking me out to breakfast."

My father knew I was right. "I'm sorry," he said. "I know I should have told you, but I was afraid you wouldn't come."

True. Very true. But I didn't admit it.

"Listen," he said. "It's still not too late for some breakfast. Why don't we go over to my apartment and I'll fix some scrambled eggs."

I couldn't let him off too easy. "No, thanks," I said. "I have a hard time eating over there."

Dad drove me home without saying another word. When I got inside, I went straight to my room. I didn't cry or anything this time, though. Instead, I took out Dr. Girard's card and looked at it.

If any of my friends ever saw it, they just wouldn't understand.

I walked to my wastebasket and tore it up.

Before I did, I memorized the number.

(ten)

TWO WEEKS after I first met Dr. Girard, it was Easter. With all the problems that were going on in my family, I had almost forgotten about it.

To tell you the truth, Easter isn't one of my favorite holidays anymore. It's better than nothing, but that's about it.

A lot of holidays seem to lose their fun when you start getting older. Easter is one of them. For me, Easter was way better when I was little. I really loved the whole Easter Bunny thing back then.

I guess there are a lot of little kids who never

take the Easter Bunny seriously. I mean, when you think about it, trying to believe that there's a giant rabbit hopping all over the world delivering eggs isn't that easy. Actually, it would probably make a lot more sense if there was an Easter Chicken. But when I was little, it didn't matter. I was one of those kids who believed whatever my parents told me. If they had told me that there was an Easter Lizard, I would have believed that, too.

When I finally found out that the Easter Bunny wasn't real, I really took it hard. And guess who told me? Good old MaryAnn Brady.

She came to school right before Easter vacation and said her mother had told her the Easter Bunny was just make-believe. She said it was really your parents who did all the basket stuff. I bet her mother *also* told her to keep that information a secret. But as you can see, even when she was little, MaryAnn was a giant blabbo.

Anyhow, when I got home that day, I ran to my mother and asked if what MaryAnn had said was true.

"Is the Easter Bunny real, or is it just pretend?" I asked.

Mom stopped what she was doing and looked at me.

"Why?" she asked. "Did someone tell you it wasn't real?"

I nodded. "MaryAnn Brady," I said. "She said her mother told her that the Easter Bunny was really your parents."

"So how do you feel about that?" my mother wanted to know. "Would you be upset if I told you that the Easter Bunny was Dad and me?"

"No," I said. "I wouldn't care a bit."

Mom smiled. "Well then, I guess that means you're old enough to understand," she said. "MaryAnn was right. The Easter Bunny is really Dad and me."

My mouth fell open.

"Oh no!" I yelled. "Oh no! Why did you have to tell me that? YOU JUST WRECKED MY WHOLE EASTER!"

My mother was stunned. "But, Charlie," she said, "you just told me that you wouldn't care."

"I lied!" I said. "I really did care. And now it's all ruined! You spoiled my whole holiday!"

I was a very weird kid. It took me a week before I finally settled down. And if you think that was bad, you should have seen me when I got the news about Santa.

Anyway, ever since then, Easter has lost most of its thrill for me. In my opinion, once you've looked in the basket and eaten the ears off the chocolate rabbit, the excitement is pretty much over.

My mother knows how I feel about Easter. But for some reason, this year she kept trying to make a big deal out of it. She kept saying stuff like, "Only six more days until Easter, Charlie."

"Am I getting a basket this year?" I asked her. "I might be getting a little old for that kind of stuff, you know."

Mom misunderstood completely. "Of course you're getting a basket," she said. "You'll never be too old for an Easter basket, Charlie. Never."

And that was that.

On the day before Easter, my mother went to the grocery store. When she came home, it looked like she had bought about a million eggs and one of those egg-dyeing kits. I'm not a big fan of coloring eggs, by the way. But since Mom had already bought the stuff, I didn't have a choice.

She boiled the eggs and called me when everything was ready. She really seemed excited about the whole operation. When I went into the kitchen, I saw that she had five cups lined up on the counter. In each cup, there was a different color dye. I decided to get right to it and get the whole thing over with.

After I had dyed one egg in each color, I started to leave.

"Is that it?" asked my mother. "Is that all you're going to do?"

"I did one in every color," I answered. "How many was I supposed to do?"

My mother went to the refrigerator and pulled out two big bowls. "I boiled three dozen eggs, Charles," she said. "You've still got thirty-one more to go."

Thirty-one more? Oh no, I thought. Not thirty-one more! What in the world were we going to do with all those eggs? I hoped my mother didn't think I was going to eat them all. I don't even like hard-boiled eggs. The yellow part is all dry and pasty, and the white part doesn't have any flavor at all.

"Why did you cook so many?" I asked.

She winked. "It's a surprise," she said. "You'll find out tomorrow. Right now, just finish coloring them."

It took me about an hour to finish dyeing all the eggs. I tried to jazz up a couple of them by putting on some stickers. Every egg-dyeing kit in the world comes with a bunch of dumb-looking stickers. Usually, they're pictures of baby chicks pushing little wheelbarrows. You've probably seen the kind I mean. They always look real cute on the front of the egg kit. But as soon as you put them on your own eggs, they bunch all up and look awful.

"Okay, I'm done," I said finally. "Is Dad coming over tomorrow? Is that the surprise?"

"No, your father's not the surprise," said Mom. "I've got something else planned."

Then she smiled and winked again.

I hate it when my mother winks at me. It was okay when I was little. In those days, I used to try and wink back. But now that I'm older, I just find it embarrassing.

When I woke up on Easter morning, I have to admit I was kind of excited. It wasn't about the Easter basket, though. I just couldn't wait to see what kind of surprise my mother had planned.

I got out of bed and hurried to the kitchen. My Easter basket was stuffed full of chocolate rabbits and jelly beans. I thanked Mom for the candy, but just as I suspected, it seemed a little babyish.

I looked all around. "So where's the big surprise?" I asked.

"It's coming later," said my mother. Then, believe it or not, she winked at me again.

"Mom?" I said. "There's something I really need to tell you. Dr. Girard said that if something bothers me, I should talk to you about it calmly and honestly."

My mother looked worried. She sat down in the chair next to me. I guess she thought it was something about the divorce.

"What is it, Charlie?" she said. "Tell me what's on your mind."

"It's just that I wish you would stop winking at me," I said. "It makes me feel ridiculous."

Mom stood back up. She didn't say anything, but she definitely looked annoyed.

"I didn't mean to make you mad," I said. "But at my age, being winked at makes me feel like a fool."

"Good. Fine. I'll never wink again," she said.

She left the room in a huff. I never realized that winking meant so much to her.

After that, the day passed pretty slowly. Time always passes slowly when you're waiting for a surprise.

By about two o'clock, I started to wonder if maybe my mother had called off the surprise completely. Maybe she was even madder about the winking than I had thought.

That's when I heard the doorbell.

"Yes! This must be it!" I said right out loud.

I ran to the front door and pulled it open.

There stood Hank.

Hank is one of my mother's cousins. She has three of them. Two of them are really cool. The other one is Hank.

We don't see Hank very often. He lives about a hundred miles away. It's what I like best about him.

Hank is a total cornball. You can tell he doesn't have any kids of his own. He's always saying the kind of stuff kids hate. You know, like calling you "little man" and junk like that.

When I saw him standing there, I was stunned for a second. I just stared.

Hank pushed his way into the house. "Hiya there, Chas!" he said loudly.

As soon as he was inside, he picked me up and swung me around.

I hate being swung around. I hate it almost as much as I hate being called Chas.

After he put me down, Hank stuck out his

hand for me to shake. "Put 'er there, big guy," he said.

I shook it.

"*Oooeee!*" he hollered. "That's really some grip you've got there, tiger!"

"I'll go get Mom," I said. Then I turned and ran full speed ahead to my mother's room. I hoped she wouldn't be upset. She usually doesn't like it when company drops by unexpectedly.

When I ran in, she had just finished fixing her hair.

"Mom, you're not going to believe this, but your crazy cousin Hank just showed up at our front door!" I said. "He's out there in the hall waiting for you!"

My mother smiled. "I know, Charlie," she said. "It's perfectly okay."

"*Whew,*" I said. "That's a relief. I thought maybe he had just dropped by or something."

"No. I knew he was coming," she said.

"Well, you better get out there and say hello," I told her. "I'm going to be in my room for a while. Call me when the surprise gets here, okay?"

Mom's face went funny. "What did you say?" she asked.

"I said, 'Call me when the surprise gets here.'"

Mom frowned. "Charlie," she said. "My cousin Hank is the surprise. He drove down to spend Easter with us."

I was hoping I hadn't heard her right.

"Hank?" I asked. "Hank is the big surprise?"

"Yes," she said. "I called him to spend the holiday here."

"But . . . but why?"

"Because I thought it would be nice if we had someone over here to share our Easter dinner with," she said.

"But why?" I asked again.

"Because I didn't want you to feel lonely," she said. "I thought we should have family around us."

"Oh," I said.

I guess I should have tried to act happier, but *oh* and *why* seemed to be all I could come up with.

Mother put her arm on my shoulder and we walked back to the hall. Hank was still there. He picked Mom up and swung her around. Then the three of us went into the living room and sat down.

"Did you get the eggs ready?" Hank asked my mother.

"Sure did," she said. "Charlie dyed them all himself."

She turned to me. "Hank had a great idea, Charles. We're going to send you on an Easter-egg hunt. That's what all the eggs were for."

"Oh," I said again.

"You're going to love this, big guy," said Hank. "When I was a boy, my parents always hid eggs in the backyard. Then my brother and I would go out and try to find them. The best thing about it was that my dad gave us money for every egg we found."

"Oh," I said, for the third time.

"Doesn't that sound like fun?" asked Mom.

Dumb. It sounded dumb. But I didn't want to hurt my mother's feelings.

"Fun," I said. "Fun."

Hank stood up and headed for the backyard. "You'll only have five minutes to find them," he said. "And here's the best part. I'm going to give you a dime for every one you find."

Whoopee, I thought.

"You stay here now, Charlie," said my mother. "Hank and I will go hide the eggs. And remember . . . no peeking."

The two of them hurried outside. I waited alone in the living room.

After a few minutes had passed, Hank called me from the back door. "OKAY, CHAS!" he shouted. "YOU CAN COME NOW! WE'RE READY!"

Slowly, I got up and walked outside. Believe me, I was in no hurry. This was one of the dumbest things I'd ever had to do in my life.

When I got outside, my mother and Hank were standing there grinning. It was obvious that they were having a lot better time than I was.

"Okay, Chas," said Hank, "you've got five minutes."

My mother shoved an empty basket in my hand. "Ten, nine, eight, seven, six, five, four, three, two, one. GO!" she shouted.

I couldn't stand how stupid she was acting.

"God, Mother," I said. "This isn't a space launch."

My mother hates it when I say *God*. I almost always get a lecture if she hears me say it. But saying *God* is as close as I can come to really swearing without serious punishment, so sometimes I say it, anyway.

This time, she ignored it.

"Just go!" she yelled. "You're wasting time! Start looking!"

Hank looked at his watch. "Hurry up, Chas," he said, "you've already wasted forty seconds."

I walked out into the middle of the yard and looked around. I spotted three eggs in the bushes. They were lying out in plain sight. Hank must have thought I needed glasses or something.

I picked them up and put them in my basket. I looked around and saw a couple more around the tree. I walked over and picked them up. Two more were balanced in the branches. I grabbed them, too.

So far I had collected seven eggs. There were twenty-nine more to go. I made my way around the yard, picking up the eggs as I walked along. Not one of them was hard to find.

Finally, Hank shouted for me to stop. "TIME'S UP!" he called. "BRING YOUR BASKET IN!"

I wished he hadn't shouted so loud. If any of my friends knew that I was hunting for eggs, I would have died. Slowly, I carried the basket over to the patio.

Mom counted them. "Thirty-six!" she said. "You got all thirty-six, Charlie! That's great!"

"Shh. Not so loud," I said.

Hank laughed. "Don't be so modest, Chas! You should be proud of yourself!" he said.

"When my brother and I used to do this, we never found all of them."

"Maybe your parents didn't put them out in plain sight," I said. "I tripped over at least ten of them."

Hank laughed again and reached into his pocket. "Let's see now. How much does old cousin Hank owe you?"

"Three-sixty," I said. I probably shouldn't have made him pay. But if you're going to make a fool out of yourself, you ought to get a little something for your effort, I think.

Hank handed me the money.

"Thanks," I said.

I turned to my mother. "Is this the end of the 'fun'?" I said. "Would it be all right if I go watch TV?"

"Sure, go ahead," she said. "Dinner will be ready in a few minutes."

I went inside and turned on the TV. Naturally, nothing good was on. No sports, no cartoons, no nothing. Television stations save their worst shows for Sunday afternoon. They probably figure that on Sunday afternoon people are so bored they'll watch anything.

They're right, too. I ended up watching this

do-it-yourself show about how to repair water rings on your tabletops.

My mother and Hank stayed outside and talked for a few minutes. When Mom came in to fix dinner, Hank flopped down beside me on the couch.

"What'cha watchin', big guy?" he asked.

I can't decide which I hate worse, *Chas* or *big guy.*

"Nothing much," I answered. "Just some dumb show."

"You mind if old Cousin Hank watches it with you?" he asked again.

I said no. But it wasn't easy. I minded a lot. The guy was seriously getting on my nerves. I thought if he called me Chas one more time, I would blow up.

"What's this show about, Chas?" he asked then.

Quickly, I sprung up from the couch. "Could you *please* stop calling me *Chas?*" I said. "I *hate* that name. How would you like me to call you Hanky? Huh? Would you like that, Cousin Hanky?"

Hank's face looked confused at first. Then just plain hurt.

"I'm sorry," he said. "I didn't know."

Right away, I felt terrible inside. I never should have shouted at him like that. Not ever.

My mother had heard me yell. She came in and grabbed me by the arm.

"Could you please excuse us for a minute, Hank?" she asked. Then she quickly pulled me down the hall to my room.

She slammed the door. "How could you, Charles?" she said. "How could you have said something so hateful?"

I didn't know myself, so I couldn't answer.

"What kind of kid are you, anyway?" she asked. "My cousin drove over a hundred miles to brighten up your Easter, and you stand there and scream at him like that? How could you?"

I shook my head.

"I don't know how I could, Mother," I said. "I'm sorry. It's just that I didn't really expect that Hank would be the big surprise today. I thought it would be something better."

"Oh, well, that's just wonderful," said Mom. "Now what am I supposed to do? Tell him he wasn't a good enough surprise and send him home? Or first, maybe you'd like to yell at him some more."

"I'm sorry," I said again.

She opened my door and pointed. "Well, don't tell me. I'm not the one who drove one hundred miles to spend Easter with you. If you're really sorry, you go tell Hank. You fix this, Charlie. I mean it."

My mother is very big on having me apologize to people. But this time, I knew she was right.

I walked back into the living room. Hank was sitting there pretending to watch the furniture show.

"Hank, I'm sorry, okay?" I said. "I'm really, really sorry for yelling at you like that. I didn't mean to make you feel bad. Honest. It's just that I've been having some personal problems lately. And I'm not really acting that good."

Hank smiled. "Don't worry about it," he said. "We all have to blow off steam once in a while. Everybody says things they don't mean."

I tried to smile back. "It's okay to call me Chas if you want," I said.

Hank reached over and ruffled my hair. "That's okay, big guy," he said.

A couple of minutes later, my mother called us to dinner. While we were eating, no one said very much. I forced myself to smile more than usual. So did my mother and Hank. It takes a while for people to start acting normal after there's been a big argument like that.

After dinner, Hank stuck around for a couple of hours. He still acted corny, but for some reason I didn't mind it as much. I guess just because someone is a big cornball, it's no reason not to like him.

I just hope that my mother doesn't think she needs to call Hank every time there's a holiday, though. If I thought his Easter-egg hunt was dumb, I'd hate to see what Hank would come up with for Halloween.

Thinking about this worried me a little. I wanted to mention it to my mother, but I didn't want her to get mad at me all over again.

Suddenly, I thought about Dr. Girard. I wondered what he might tell me to do?

There was only one way to find out.

I went to the phone and dialed his number.

The voice on the other end was a recording. It said: "Dr. Girard is not in the office right now. At the sound of the tone, please leave your name and telephone number, and Dr. Girard will return your call . . . *beep!*"

"This is Charles Hickle, Dr. Girard," I said

nervously. "My number is 555-6788. Please call me back. Thanks."

After I hung up, I already felt better. Just the idea that there was someone I could talk to helped me more than I thought.

(eleven)

S O FAR, I've talked to Dr. Girard four times. Each time he's made me feel a little bit better about things.

Don't get me wrong, though. I still don't think I'm ever going to totally get over this. And I still think divorce is a rotten thing for parents to do.

It's really hard for me to get used to living just with my mother. It must be weird for her, too. Almost every night, when she sets the table, she accidentally puts out three plates.

Once in a while, Mom calls me "the man of the house." I don't know if she's trying to make me feel grown-up or what. But I don't really like it. Just because they decided to get divorced doesn't suddenly turn me into a man. I don't even shave yet. The next thing you know, she'll expect me to go to work or something.

Of course, maybe going to work wouldn't be so bad. It's got to be better than school. Because to tell you the truth, school hasn't been going that well for me lately. I used to be pretty good in school, but ever since the divorce, I've had a hard time keeping my mind on stuff. Somehow, learning how brine shrimp lay eggs just doesn't seem important anymore.

Right after my teacher found out that things were bad for me at home, she got real nice. She didn't make me do any work at all, hardly. But teachers don't stay patient like that forever. Teachers definitely have a limit on their niceness.

Last Friday after school, Mrs. Fensel handed me a note to take home to my mother. She told me to be sure that Mom saw it.

"I'm going to trust you not to read it first, Charles," she said.

What a lie. If she really "trusted me not to read it," why did she have it all sealed up with tape? Does that sound like trust to you?

Having to take a note home to your mother is

one of the worst things a kid ever has to do. It's like asking a criminal to cut off his own head, sort of. It's just not fair.

All the way home I held the note real loosely in my hand. I kept waiting for a big strong gust of wind to come along and blow it away. But as usual, there's never a good wind when you need one.

The same thing used to happen when I was a little kid and I wanted to fly my kite. I would spend about an hour untangling my ball of string, and by the time I got it all ready, the wind had totally stopped. Usually, I ended up dragging it up and down the street a couple of times and putting it away.

The only time it's ever windy is when you don't want it to be. Like when you finish swimming, for instance. I don't know where the wind comes from, but as soon as you get out of the water, a big gust comes and freezes your tail off.

Anyhow, on the day Mrs. Fensel gave me the note, the wind was nowhere to be found. I tried blowing it away myself by sneezing on it really hard. But that didn't work, either. I think all the tape was weighing it down.

When I finally got home, I decided to take the note to my room first before giving it to my mother. I thought that maybe I could hold it up to the light and read a few words. But when I looked through the envelope, all I could see was that the note was folded into a tiny little wad. Good old Mrs. Fensel. She knew every trick in the book.

The stupid thing was, I really didn't need to read the note at all. I knew exactly what it was going to say. And trust me, Mom wasn't going to be too thrilled about it.

My grades hadn't been very good lately. In fact, the highest mark I had gotten that week was a D+ in spelling. I would have gotten a C−, but I forgot to capitalize Russia.

Personally, I think it's really stupid to count a word wrong just because you didn't use a capital. It's not that you're using the wrong letter, it's just that you've used it in an alternative size.

As I stood there with that note, I thought about how much trouble I was going to be in. For the first time in five weeks, I began to think about running away from home again. When it comes to getting good grades, my mother is really tough.

I knew exactly what she would do. She would read the note and then call me into the living room for a little "talk." And if there's one thing that I hate, it's one of my mother's little "talks" about schoolwork.

First, she starts out by telling me how she isn't going to yell or scold me. Then she yells and scolds me. After that, she starts taking away all of the fun things that I like to do and tries to make it seem like it's for my "own good." That way, she doesn't feel so mean.

The more I thought about it, the dumber it seemed to actually give Mom the note at all. I mean, if I already knew what she was going to say, what was the point of bothering her with it? Instead, I could give myself my own little "talk" and save her the trouble.

"Okay," I said to myself. "I promise that I'll watch less TV and study harder."

There. Now my poor mother wouldn't have to feel so mean about yelling at me. What a thoughtful son I was to spare her that.

Besides, Mrs. Fensel hadn't specifically told me to *give* my mother the note. All she had said to do was to be sure Mom *saw* it. So, if my mother saw the envelope, I wouldn't be doing anything wrong.

Mom was in the kitchen. I grabbed the note and went in to say hello.

We talked for a while about the usual stuff. Then finally, I headed for my room again. Right before I left the kitchen, I dropped the note on the floor.

I picked it right up and kept on going.

"What was that?" asked my mother.

"Nothing," I called from the hall. "It's just a note that someone wrote at school. No big deal."

When I got back to my room, I felt much better. Now I wouldn't be lying when I told Mrs. Fensel that my mother saw the note. There's no doubt about it . . . I am definitely a clever kid.

Now that the matter was settled, there really wasn't any reason why I couldn't open the note and read it. No one would ever know. And I was really dying to see what Mrs. Fensel had written about me.

I tried to tear open the envelope with my hands but the tape was too thick. "Is this what you call trust, Mrs. Fensel?" I growled.

Finally, I managed to slit open the bottom of the envelope with my pen. I pulled the note out and began reading:

Dear Mrs. Hickle,

This note is to let you know that your son, Charles, has been doing very poorly with his schoolwork. In the past week, he has had no grade higher than a D+.

Mrs. Hickle, I do understand that Charles has been having some problems at home, and I have tried to be understanding. But he's still not paying attention in class, so I feel it's time I let you know what is happening.

In addition to his grades, his behavior has also taken a turn for the worse. Charles used to be a very well behaved boy. Lately, however, he has started to become rather rude, both to me and to others in the classroom.

I would appreciate any effort that you and his father would make to see that Charles changes both his behavior and his grades. If all of us work together, I'm sure we can get him back on the right track.

Sincerely,
Edna Fensel

Rude? I couldn't believe it! She actually told my mother that I was *rude*.

What's so rude about telling a teacher that you think spelling stinks? Especially when it's the truth. And especially when Mrs. Fensel started the whole conversation herself.

After I got my last spelling test back, she came over to my desk and asked me what was wrong with my spelling lately.

"Nothing is wrong with my spelling," I said. "The reason I got a D is because you marked 'russia' wrong. I spelled 'russia' right."

She looked at my paper.

"Russia has a capital," she said.

"I know," I said. "The capital of Russia is Moscow."

Mrs. Fensel didn't laugh at my joke. She pretended she didn't even hear it, in fact.

"If you don't spell Russia with a capital, it's wrong," she said.

That's when I said, "Spelling stinks."

"Pardon me?" said Mrs. Fensel.

"Stinks. S-T-I-N-K-S," I spelled.

Mrs. Fensel gave me an angry look. At first, I didn't think she was going to do anything more. But instead of yelling at me, she wrote that note to my mother. What a squealer. A guy makes a couple of amusing comments, and boom . . . he gets a note sent home.

Anyway, after I read the note, I was very glad I hadn't shown it to my mother. At least I was glad until about 8:30 that night. At 8:30, I stopped being glad about a lot of things. That's when Mrs. Fensel called.

I was in the shower when the phone rang. But after I got out, I could hear my mother talking. It didn't take a genius to figure out who she was talking to. She kept saying stuff like "Yes, Mrs. Fensel, I know he's having a hard time." And "No, Mrs. Fensel, I don't know why he didn't show it to me."

I was doomed.

Wait.

Or *was* I?

An idea popped into my head that just might work.

I threw on my pajamas and ran into my room to get the note. I decided not to put it back in its torn-up envelope. I thought it might look suspicious. So I just folded it up and ran to my mother. She had just hung up the phone.

"Oh, wow, Mom," I said. "I almost forgot to give you this note. I just thought about it while I was in the shower. It's from Mrs. Fensel."

My mother grabbed the note out of my hand and read it. She had this look on her face like she was about to explode.

After she finished reading, her expression

changed. She got a funny grin. It wasn't what you'd call a happy grin, though. It was more like the kind of grin that insane people have on TV shows.

She began walking toward me very slowly. It really made me nervous. I started backing up. I backed all the way into the wall. She had me cornered.

My mother leaned real close to me. Then she put her hands on my shoulders and began talking very softly.

"Charles," she said, "I'm going to give you three weeks. That's three," she repeated, as she held up her fingers. "One . . . two . . . three. And if at the end of three weeks, your grades aren't back up to where they are supposed to be, you are going to be one very unhappy boy."

I looked at her face. The insane grin was still there.

I gulped. "What do you mean? What will happen to me?" I asked.

"Oh . . . let's see. Do you want a little hint?" Mom said. "I'll give you lots of little hints."

She started right in.

"Little hint number one, no TV. Little hint number two, no sports. Little hint number three, no having friends over. Little hint number four, no *telephone*. Little hint number five, *no CD player*. Little hint number six, *no computer games*. Little hint number seven, *no allowance*. Are you getting the picture yet, Charlie?" she asked.

"Yes," I said. "At least, mostly I am. It's just that I don't exactly understand little hint number seven. I mean, I get the ones about no TV and stuff, because I'll have to study more. But what does my allowance have to do with my schoolwork?"

I wasn't trying to make her angrier, I swear. I just really wanted to know about the allowance thing.

Mom cleared it up. "Oh, you won't need any money, Charlie," she explained. "Because you won't be setting foot out of this house for a very . . . long . . . time. Get it?"

"Got it," I said. "Can I go now?"

"Just one more teensy little thing," said my mother. "If I ever again hear that you've been rude to your teacher, I will personally take you by the hand and lead you to your classroom, where you will apologize to Mrs. Fensel in front of everyone. Do you get that, too?"

I nodded. This was definitely something that my mother would do. Like I mentioned before, she's very big on apologizing.

When I was little, I accidentally called this old lady down the street a dirtbag. I didn't even know what a dirtbag was, really. But I was trying to make some kids laugh. So when we rode by her on my bike, I hollered, "Hi there, dirtbag."

The lady found out who I was and called my mother. The next day, Mom took me down there and made me tell the dirtbag I was sorry for calling her names.

The point is, I could just see my mother leading me into my classroom and making me apologize for being a smart aleck. She'd love it.

"Are you going to tell Dad about this?" I asked. "Because, well, I was just thinking . . . maybe we could keep this our own little secret. I mean, really, Mom. There's no need bothering Dad with it, is there? After all, he's got his own trouble trying to live in that stinky apartment. What do you say? Is it a deal?"

My mother didn't answer.

She was already in the kitchen dialing my father's number.

(twelve)

YESTERDAY WAS my eleventh birthday. I wish I had a chance to do it over again. I really blew it. In fact, it was the worst birthday I've ever had in my life. It was even worse than the one when I asked for a real bow-and-arrow set and got the kind with the rubber suction cups on the ends.

This time, it wasn't the presents that made my birthday crummy, though. In fact, this time I got exactly what I asked for. I just wish I had asked for something else.

I have to admit, from the very beginning, Mom had tried to talk me out of it. But after I kept on begging, she finally gave in. Sometimes,

I wish my mother was a little bit stronger person.

A week before my birthday, I cornered her in the kitchen.

"My birthday's coming up, you know," I said. "Isn't it about time you started thinking about it?"

Mom's hand flew over her mouth.

"Oh my gosh. You're right," she said. Then she sat down in the kitchen chair and put her head down on the table.

After about ten seconds, she raised up.

"Okay, I'm finished thinking about it," she said. "Can I get up now?"

"That's not funny," I said. "Aren't you even going to ask me what I want?"

She walked over and put her hands on my shoulders.

"I haven't let you down yet, have I?" she asked.

"What about the time you gave me the arrows with the rubber suction cups on the ends?" I said.

She laughed. "Oh, yeah. I forgot about that one," she said. "Okay. You win. What do you want for your birthday?"

I took a deep breath. I had known what I

wanted ever since my dad left. I had a feeling my mother wasn't going to like the idea much. But there was only one way to find out.

"I want to go on a picnic with you and Dad," I said. Then I closed my eyes and waited for her to say no.

But Mom surprised me. "I was expecting something like that," she said.

My face brightened. "Really? So does that mean we can do it?" I asked.

"Of course we can't do it," she said. "Think of something else."

"No, Mother. *Please*. I want a picnic," I begged. "Just one crummy picnic. Can't you and Dad just do me this one little favor and take your poor son on a picnic? I think it's the least you can do. After all, you are ruining my life, you know. I really don't think that one little picnic will kill you."

Mom thought a second. "We'll compromise," she said. "I'll invite your father over, and the two of you can eat cake on a blanket in the living room."

"Not funny," I said.

"Neither is the thought of going on a picnic with your dad," she said. "And believe me,

Charlie, he won't like the idea any better than I do."

"But what if he says yes?" I asked. "If Dad says yes, will you go?"

"He's not going to say yes," she said.

"But if he *does*, will you go?" I asked again.

My mother finally gave in. "Oh, all right," she said. "I'll go if your father goes. But the only reason I'm agreeing to it is because I'm positive that he'll never say yes. I know your dad pretty well, Charlie. You can't live with someone for this many years and not know them."

Maybe that was one of my parents' big problems. Maybe they didn't know each other as well as they thought they did.

My father said yes right away. He even acted happy about it.

"Sure, I'll go on a picnic," he said. "It'll be fun."

"Great!" I said happily. "Mom said you wouldn't want to go. She said that she was positive that you'd hate the idea."

"That's ridiculous," said Dad. "There is no reason in the world why we can't take you on a picnic for your birthday. Your mother and I are two grown-up people. We don't go around fighting like a couple of little kids. I'm sure we can still all have a nice time together. Tell her I'll pick you up at noon on Saturday."

"Perfect," I told him.

I had a feeling that the real reason my father wanted to go on a picnic was just to get out of his apartment. I was sure that by now, the stink had started to get to him. But it didn't matter to me why he wanted to go. All I knew was that the three of us would be together again.

"Dad's going! He's going on the picnic!" I shouted as I walked in the house that afternoon. "He thought the picnic was a great idea!"

You should have seen Mom's face when she heard the news. Her mouth went all weird, like she had just eaten something that tasted bad.

"Are you sure he knows that I'm going, too?" she asked.

"Positive," I answered. "He said that you're both adults and you should be able to have a nice time together. He also said that he'd pick us up at noon on Saturday."

"Hurray," she said dryly. "I can hardly wait."

By the time Saturday came, I couldn't wait, either. I kept hoping that if all of us had a good time together, my parents would see what a terrible mistake they were making. I hoped that the picnic might turn things around for us, so that we could be a family again.

I also hoped that my mother really didn't think I meant it when I said that all I wanted for my birthday was a picnic. I definitely wanted presents, too. That may sound kind of greedy, but let's face it, your birthday only comes once a year.

When my father came to pick us up, Mom opened the truck door for me. But instead of getting in, I bent down and pretended to tie my shoe. My mother stood there for a minute and then got in herself. I slid in beside her and closed the door. I thought that maybe if the two of them sat together, they would begin to get that old "married feeling" again.

Unfortunately, they didn't even smile at each other or say hello. All Mom did was keep squeezing over toward my side, making me real uncomfortable. Every time we went over a bump, the picnic basket on her lap poked into my side. Luckily, the park wasn't too far away.

When we got there, I grabbed the blanket and ran to find us a perfect spot to sit down. I decided on a place right next to the lake. It was really pretty there.

As soon as my parents caught up with me, my

mother sat down on the blanket and started opening up the basket of food.

"No, wait. Hold it," I said. "We're not supposed to eat yet. We usually play Frisbee to work up an appetite first."

"I've never really liked to play Frisbee," said my mother. "I always break my fingernails when I catch it."

Dad grinned. "How could that be? You never catch it," he said.

"I do so," Mom snapped. "The only time I don't catch it is when you whiz it at me at ninety miles an hour."

"Don't be a sissy," said Dad. "Come on, let's play."

My mother stood up. "Frisbee," she said, under her breath. "Even the name of it sounds dumb."

Dad got the Frisbee out of the truck. On his way back, he tossed it to me. I caught it and threw it back.

When he got closer, he tossed it to my mother. It hit her in the head.

"Okay, that's it. I'm not playing anymore," she said.

She went to the blanket and started pulling all the food out of the picnic basket.

"It's time to eat," she called. "If you don't come now, the flies will get it."

I went over and bent down next to her. "You're not acting very grown-up about this," I said quietly.

She told me to shut up. Seriously. She actually said to *shut up* on my birthday.

Things were tenser than I thought.

My father grabbed a sandwich. "What kind is it?" he asked.

"Liverwurst," said my mother.

Dad made a sick face. "Liverwurst? I *hate* liverwurst," he said.

Mom smiled. "Yes, I know," she said.

Things weren't going at all like I had hoped. In fact, I didn't think they could get any worse. But I was wrong.

While we were eating, a woman and two chubby toddlers came walking toward us. The woman was carrying a blanket and a grocery bag. When she got about three feet from us, she smiled and spread her blanket right next to ours.

I couldn't believe my eyes. I mean, the whole park was practically empty, and she had to sit directly next to us.

But that's not even the worst part. The worst

part is that the little kids had no manners at all. As soon as their blanket was ready, they plopped down and started to stare.

Dad said to ignore them, but it wasn't easy. They were the rudest kids I had ever seen. I hate being stared at. I tried staring back, but it didn't work. Little kids can go forever without looking away.

After we had finished eating, my father went to the truck again. He came back with an armful of gifts. Man, you should have seen the kids then! They started acting like they were at my birthday party or something.

Their mother did, too. "Ooooh, are you a birthday boy?" she said.

The older kid pointed to one of my presents. "I bet that's a football. Look how it's wrapped. You can tell."

I could see that this made my father mad. It was his present. He'd wrapped it himself. He turned around and told the kid to "please be quiet."

Before I opened anything, my mother passed out cupcakes to Dad and me. As soon as she got them out of the box, the littlest kid waddled right onto our blanket.

"Me want cupcake, too," he said.

His mother laughed.

My mother didn't. "I only have three," she said, kind of grouchy.

The kid stamped his foot. "Barney want cupcake. Barney want cupcake!" he hollered.

"Go on," said Mom. "You look like you've had too many cupcakes already."

When she heard that, the kid's mother stopped laughing. "He's just a baby," she said.

Meanwhile, the kid was still screaming. "Barney want cupcake!"

By this time, my mother had really had it. She leaned real close to the kid's face and shouted, "No! No cupcake!"

I guess she must have scared him. The kid jumped about a foot and fell over our blanket. He started crying as loud as he could.

His mother came over and picked him up. "It's people like you who make children afraid of strangers," she said.

Then she grabbed her blanket and stomped off.

The other little kid stood there a second. "Meanie!" he said.

My mother was even angrier than I thought. I could hardly believe what she said next.

"Go home, brat boy!" she hollered.

The kid turned and ran.

I still can't believe she said that. Let's face it. "Go home, brat boy" is not something that mothers usually say.

My father and I both stared at her.

"Well, I'm sorry," she said. "But he was getting on my nerves."

"For heaven's sake," said Dad. "He was just a little kid."

"I *said* I was sorry," snapped my mother. "Let's just forget about it."

She turned to me. "Well, are you going to open up your presents or not?"

"Yeah, sure," I said.

"Which one do you want to open first?" asked my father.

"The football," I said.

Dad handed me the package. I could tell he was still mad about it.

"How do you know it's a football?" he asked. "Just because that little kid said so, doesn't mean it's a football. It could be anything."

I opened it up.

It was a football.

I opened up the rest of the presents. Mom had bought me some CDs and a boom box for my room. My father gave me the football and two computer games.

After I had thanked them, we all piled into the truck and drove home. This time, I sat in the middle. It was a lot more comfortable that way.

When we got there, Mom and I got out of the truck. I started to walk around to say good-bye to my father. But as it turned out, I didn't have to. He was already on his way to the house. I guess he just didn't want to leave me on my birthday.

I have to admit, when I saw him going in the front door, it really surprised me. It must have surprised my mother, too. Before either of us knew it, Dad had sat down on the couch.

My mother crossed her arms.

"Won't you sit down?" she asked.

My father smiled. This whole situation was stressing me out. Having them together at the picnic had turned out to be bad enough. But being inside the house with them was even worse. I knew that, sooner or later, an argument was going to get started.

I wasn't quite sure what I should do. Finally, I sat down on the couch next to Dad.

Mom didn't know what to do, either. For a while, she walked around pretending to be busy. Then she gave up and sat down in the chair across from us.

For a long time, no one said a word. It was worse than the dinner with Cousin Hank. We all just sat there looking at the floor. All I could hear was the sound of my father's watch ticking. Tick-tick-tick . . .

It reminded me of this TV show I saw one time. It was about these two policemen who had to take the fuse out of a time bomb so it wouldn't explode. It really got tense at the end. They had to work very slowly so they wouldn't accidentally set it off. But the whole time they were working, all you could hear was the tick-tick-tick of the time bomb . . . just like my father's watch.

All of a sudden, I couldn't stand the silence anymore. I tried to start a conversation.

"So, did you guys have a nice time today?" I asked.

It was probably the worst question I could have asked.

"I did," said Dad. "It was really fun, wasn't it? I especially liked tossing around the old Frisbee."

My mother glared. "I liked the liverwurst," she said.

Okay. That did it.

"Excuse me," I said. "I'll be right back."

I left the room and hurried down the hall. I went straight to Mom's bedroom and called Dr. Girard. His secretary said he was busy on the other line.

"Yeah, but this is an emergency," I said in my loudest whisper. "I really need to talk to him now."

Dr. Girard picked up the phone right away.

I told him what was going on.

We didn't talk long. We didn't have to. The answer to my problem turned out to be so simple, I should have known it myself.

When I got off the phone, I went back to the living room and sat down next to Dad again. Only this time, I sat extra close.

"I need to tell you something private," I said softly.

My father leaned his head over in my direction.

I cupped my hands around his ear.

"Could you please go home?" I whispered.

Dad sat there a second; then he smiled a little. Dr. Girard said he would understand.

He got up and said good-bye to my mother.

I walked him to the door. When we got there, he bent down and gave me a hug.

"I guess sometimes adults aren't quite as grown-up as they think they are," he said.

He hugged me again and left.

(thirteen)

TODAY IS Sunday. Dad just called. He's going to stop by later on and pick me up. We're going over to his place and toss around my new football.

I don't mind going over there quite as much anymore. He's painted the walls and bought himself a new couch to replace the smelly one.

For a joke, he bought me a can of rose-scented bathroom spray. He lets me spray the room before I sit down.

It's funny, but there have been times lately when I've begun to think of him as more than just my father. There have been times when he's started to seem like someone I might actually like to hang out with.

My mother still seems exactly like my mother. But maybe that will be changing, too. The other day she told me that she's looking for a job.

When I first heard her say it, I started laughing. I think I hurt her feelings. I didn't mean to. It's just that she's always been a stay-at-home mom, so it's hard for me to think of her as a working person.

I talked to Dr. Girard about it. He told me that when his parents got divorced, his mother became a mailman.

I must have laughed for about ten minutes when he said that. I don't know why, but the thought of my mother becoming a mailman really kills me.

Dr. Girard is a pretty funny guy.

Sometimes I think back to when I first met him. It seems like a long time ago, but it's only been a couple of months.

I think I've come a long way in two months. I don't go around happy all the time, but I'm not sad as much, either.

I guess nothing can keep you sad forever. Forever is just too long.

It's like that bicycle I told you about earlier. As you stand there and watch it get run over, you get this real sick feeling inside. But after a while, you realize that if you save your money, you can get another one. It may take some time, but you can do it.

And even though the second bike may be different from the first one, you can still be happy with it. Just because it's different doesn't make it bad.

I guess that's what I'm trying to do now. I'm trying to be happy with something different. I know it's going to take time before I feel like my old self again. But at least I think I'm getting closer.

Like take today, for instance. When I walked by my mirror this morning, I caught myself smiling.

And no one even had to ask.

Find out what happens to Charlie Hickle next in

My Mother Got Married (And Other Disasters)

Another bummer!

Charlie Hickle's life has become a three-ring circus. It was bad enough that Charlie's parents got divorced. Now, to make matters worse, Charlie's mom is getting remarried, and suddenly there are *way* too many people in one house. First there's his new stepfather, the nature guy. Then there's his five-year-old stepbrother, Thomas the pest, who's Charlie's new roommate. Worst of all, Charlie has to deal with his stepsister, Lydia the phone-hog. His mom promises that things will work out eventually.

But Charlie isn't interested in *eventually*. He wants things back the way they used to be—*right now!*

BarBara ParK is one of today's funniest, most popular authors. Her middle-grade novels have won more than forty children's book awards. She is also the creator of the hilarious Junie B. Jones series. Barbara holds a BS in education from the University of Alabama. She has two grown sons and lives with her husband, Richard, in Arizona.